Vanilla's Ladies

A Woman Running a Man's Game

Emilia Szleszynska

iUniverse, Inc.
Bloomington

Vanilla's Ladies
A Woman Running a Man's Game

iUniverse books may be ordered through booksellers or by contacting:

iUniverse
1663 Liberty Drive
Bloomington, IN 47403
www.iuniverse.com
1-800-Authors (1-800-288-4677)

Because of the dynamic nature of the Internet, any Web addresses or links contained in this book may have changed since publication and may no longer be valid. The views expressed in this work are solely those of the author and do not necessarily reflect the views of the publisher, and the publisher hereby disclaims any responsibility for them.

Any people depicted in stock imagery provided by Thinkstock are models, and such images are being used for illustrative purposes only.

Special thanx to Jason Clavey for the photography, Lyndsay Morrison for the grammar and spelling check, my self Emilia Szleszynska for the cover design and photo shoot directory, my beautiful friends and models Yassii, Nicole, Salma, Raylin, Far for the support. And my good friends Claudia Melo Lane and Hannah Morgan from Beauty Box for the wonderful make up job they done on my models for my book cover shoot x.

Certain stock imagery © Thinkstock.

ISBN: 978-1-4502-8102-7 (sc)
ISBN: 978-1-4502-8288-8 (hc)
ISBN: 978-1-4502-8104-1 (ebk)

Library of Congress Control Number: 2010918926

Printed in the United States of America

iUniverse rev. date: 03/14/2012

Dedication

I can't believe I have done this! First person comes to mind is my munchkin Nadia Iqbal. Thank you for sitting here with me one night in my little cottage in Juniper Green and telling me straight to my face to get my manuscript published what the hell am i waiting for? I did it baby! And i know you and the girls are proud of mc. Shivon Prakash, M.C. Thom,Claudia Melo-Lane,Leighan Pearson, Mrs. Jackqui Iqbal, Donna Kaur,Sammi Eddie, you all hold a special place in my heart.

I can't forget my wonderful family my mother Irena Szleszynska, my daddy Marian Szleszynski and my sisters Aneta Marzouq and Magdalena Szleszynska and my beautiful niece Tiffany. Auntie loves you baby. Mostly I want to say thank you to my partner Neil, step daughter Laurie and our little girl Chloe Alexandra for making my life complete .Also to my partners new family for making me one of there own. I love you very much and I know you are proud of me. Family is so important and I'm glad I have you in my life.

Can't forget my wonderful grandparents Jadwiga and Alexander Kurzadkowsi(R.I.P) not a day goes by that I don't think of you. You were my world when I was a child. Love you, see you in heaven.

Big thanx to my family in Poland for being there for me when I moved back. Even though I have not been a perfect Christian I want to thank my God Jesus Christ for keeping me strong through all my trials and tribulations.

There is a lot of other people who made a important impact on my life I can't name you all in here, but you know who you are. Those that know me they know how, where and why I wrote Vanilla's Ladies. I decided to make it come a live in Edinburgh, Scotland. Dreams do come true so don't give up on yours! Thank you all for the support and believing in me. God bless

Detroit

Michigan

To all my

Money getting

woman

The client had already told me how much he'd paid, but I ask Nikki anyway.

"Nine-hundred for the hour," she says.

Good girl, at least she's being honest.

"Give me $600," I say, "and keep the rest."

"Give you $600?" Nikki sounds shocked.

I know she's not trying to check me! I give the bitch a piece of my mind.

"What the hell do you expect? I hook this shit up! I pay for the hotel room, for the ads, the damn phone bill! I take the chance to put money in *your* hands! I'm doing you a favour, if you don't like it, go and let one of those so-called pimps put you on the hoe stroll then!

"It's not like you're walking the streets at night on Michigan Avenue or Woodward, you're laid up in a five point star hotel complaining and shit! Other hoes wish they were in your shoes!

"I don't tell you what to do in your personal life. I don't tell you where to go or who to have sex with on your own time, as long as you do what you're supposed to do on my time! You don't like it, you can leave right now. It'll take you all day if not longer to make $300 after you've sucked about five dicks on the hoe stroll. I could really be pimping you and taking *all* your money!"

I only stop yelling because the phone rings. Saved by the bell. I tell Nikki to pick it up.

"Hello?"

"Yes, she's here, may I ask who is calling?"

"It's Spin." She gives me the phone and walks through to the other room.

"Hey Vanilla babe, I miss you. Can I come over?" Spin asks me as soon as I say hello.

"I'm taking care of business right now, plus I need you over there, I've got some more clients for you this afternoon, so just relax and make some money." Any excuse to keep her from coming over here.

"Whatever Vanilla, I'll see you later!" She sounds a little mad, so I'll say anything to keep her happy. "Spin, you know I love you, right?"

I say that to her every time I want to calm her ass down.

"Yeah, that's what your mouth says every time you're up to no good, V."

"I'll holla at you later."

She slams the receiver down.

I hang up and call for Nikki. She walks into the room looking sexy as hell and sits on my lap. I rub her pretty mocha face, looking into those deep hazel eyes. I rub her soft legs; run my hands through her beautiful honey blonde and red hair; move her face closer to mine and softly kiss her sexy lips. She looks up at me and smiles, revealing those pretty white teeth, but she messes up the moment by asking who Spin is. I make the answer short and sweet.

"Don't worry about that, just do what you've got to do and you'll be taken care of." I kiss her again and once more I am interrupted by the phone.

I book her another call; this time it's a casino call, $1,500. I tell her to keep $500 and give me a 'G' and she says OK. She pushes me back on the bed and kisses me passionately. I smile to myself and know where this is heading.

While she is busy giving me some of the best head I've ever had, I think about Spin. She can't find out about Nikki, she will kill the poor girl. I'm not worried about the others, Spin is my dime piece, but Nikki might have her beat. My goal is to keep them away from each other. I can't fuck up my money over any pussy! That's a no-no.

Chapter 1:
_____

It's about 9.15pm. I'm on Telegraph about to hit the mile (7-mile) listening to my boy Trick Trick, in my pink 2009 DTs Caddy. The 15s (speakers) are banging while the 24s are spinning. I've got a bottle of Rose Label Moet between my legs, a Newport in one hand, my cell phone in the other, driving with my knees. I get caught by the lights.

Some cats in an Escalade try to halla, I turn my radio up; I don't have time for play. I'm trying to get to Spin and get to my money, which is way more important. I raise the bottle up to them, smile and take a sip. They laugh and I pull off. I lose them and hit the Lodge freeway, enjoying this beautiful day in the city.

It's June 2009 and, like I said before, it is a beautiful day in the city. I grew up on the west side of Detroit, Michigan. The Motor City, Mo-Town; it's ugly, but beautiful at the same time. It is my home, my city, and I do love it.

I'm on my way to see my wife, Spin, and pick up my money from the other girls. Money always come first, then pleasure. I pull up at the hotel. Fifteen minutes later she comes out the room. She looks more beautiful every time I see her, with her Gucci bag and that sexy ass iceberg dress that shows off all her perfect curves. Damn she looks good! She gets in and gives me a kiss. I tell her she looks beautiful and she says the same to me. She starts playing with my CD player. I slap her hand. She laughs. She knows how I am about my radio. Do not fuck with my music!

I take the CD out. My boy Trick Trick has some sweet tracks on there. I've got to show the home town some love. I like all kinds of music. At this moment I'm in the mood for a little Trina. I play my favourite track, *That's just my attitude*, and really mean it. I hit the freeway on my way to pick up my drops from the other girls.

Let me introduce myself. My name is "Vanilla"; well, that is what people call me. I'm a 19 year old white female, 5'3", 130 pounds, 36C, no kids. I'm not legally married since same sex marriage is not yet legal in the State of Michigan. I'm a blond with green-blue eyes, not bad looking from what I've been told.

I have a beautiful older sister; she's the good one in the family. My parents are my pride and joy. I grew up in the church, but like a lot of baby Christians I backslid and thought I was bigger than God. I was money hungry and wanted so much more from life. But, like a lot of people, I didn't want to work too hard for it. So I decided to get rich the easy way.

My biggest weakness is my wife, Spin. But since she is my partner in crime, we make our money together. I own my own escort service; it's called *Vanilla's Ladies*. I don't call myself a Madam, I call myself a businesswoman. After all, I do pay taxes (now at least), well, some of them. I don't like being compared to a pimp. To me, pimps are dirty, broke, down ass niggas who use women.

Me, I love women! I love to help them get on their own two feet so they will have something in life. And, of course, I help myself. I try my best to treat them with respect. I don't put them on the hoe stroll. They are all in five point star hotels doing business with high class clients; doctors, lawyers, judges, etc… rich men who will pay top dollar for some fine pussy. All my girls are dime pieces. They are not crack heads sucking dick for a $20.00 crack rock or less. Most of them are in college. They are not just pretty hoes, they are smart hoes too. You can't get any better than that.

I advertise my girls on the internet, in the Metro Times, the Detroit Free Press, and the Yellow Pages. They do everything from sex, to cooking and cleaning. I call my girls the wifeys, because they do everything a wife can do, from being a freak to being a house wife. They have wifey credentials. So far I've got six girls working for me. I need one more; I always wanted a hoe for every day of the week. That way I'll never get bored.

I had seven, but this bitch named Tammi didn't know how to act. The bitch stole from me, and then tried to lie about it at that! So I waited about two weeks and let the bitch make about 20 Grand, knowing the dumb hoe was keeping the money in the hotel room she was staying in. I sent some of my hood niggas over there and they took every dime the hoe had on her, as well as her clothes and jewellery. They left her ass there butt naked. I called the hoe and told her she can't steal from me and get away with it. I also told her not to even think about trying to work for any other service in the city, because I run this shit! I hung up on the bitch, and have not seen her since.

My other four girls' names are Diamond, Destiny, Sophia and Suhey.

Suhey is mixed, Puerto Rican and Black. I call her my Caramel Crème. She's 5'7", 145 pounds, has green-blue eyes, beautiful jet black hair, and the sweetest smile you've ever seen. She's all class, no trash.

Diamond is my gorgeous white chick; a hot blonde bombshell. She used to model and she thinks she's as hot as Lisa Ray on *Players Club*. She's fine alright, but she's no Lisa Ray! I don't dare tell her that though. She favours her, just a white version of her.

Destiny is every man's dream; a beautiful cream-complexioned queen. She has the prettiest sky-blue eyes and the juiciest Angelina Jolie lips you will ever find on a white girl. Her carrot red hair really makes her cream complexion shine. And I can't forget the J. Lo. Booty. Plus she is smart as hell!

Now Sophia is a Mexicana with too much mouth, but that's why I like her so much. She's my 'ride and die' chick. She's a Chicana with a big booty, big titties, brown skin, big brown eyes, wavy black hair half way down her back, and she's thick in all the right places. That's the only woman Spin knows about me having sex with since we have our threesomes with her.

Now let me tell you about my Queen Bee, "Miss Spin" herself. She is the finest thing that God has ever made, in my eyes. My baby looks like my bitch Beyonce - to me at least. And if you know me, you know I'm crazy in love with that beautiful sista! Spin's 5'10", 155 pounds, with a Coke bottle shape, and hazel eyes. She's my bootylicious black beauty queen. She has eyes the shape of almonds, and titties and nipples so pretty I can't keep my eyes, hands, or mouth off them.

Plus she's my no.1 hustler, can't get better than that either. She's my wifey, my bitch, my everything. At the age of 24 she has accomplished a lot. My baby is due to graduate from Law School in about two years. She's got her own crib, cars, even a little real estate; thanks to me of course. She knows that without my help she wouldn't have shit. She just needed a little guidance as to how to make her money. We made a promise to each other that once she is finished with University we're going to give this shit up. That way, I can concentrate on getting my degree in Business Management, and I can open my own strip club. You can't be a hoe for life. I'm stacking my paper for the future, so when I'm ready to open my own club, I won't have anything to worry about.

Spin has been with me since I started my escort service at the age of 16. You may be asking 'how did I get into all of that?' All I'm going to say is that the internet is a beautiful thing. Spin was my first working girl. I met her at the titty bar. Same place I met all my other girls. Different titty bars, but the girls were all, more or less, in the same line of work; looking for someone to save them, and I was Capitan-save-a-hoe.

If you're wondering what the hell I was doing at a titty bar, well I've been going there since I was 14 years old. You've just got to know the right people to get into the right places. Age is nothing but a number if you've got money, or a mouthpiece. Back then I had a mouthpiece only, now I've got both. Life is good - for some of us at least. My girls don't consider themselves hoes; they prefer 'professional call girls'. What's the difference? They make ten times the money, plus everything is done with class. Some of them don't know what to do with the money, some do. But it's none of my business what they do with it after I get my cut.

Spin is the only one that keeps 70% of her money; since she is my other half, I show her a little more love. She knows who runs this shit though. She's very jealous, but that's why I love her so much. Nikki on the other hand is special, there's something about her. She's obedient, I love that. I've got to keep them away from each other.

I know you are probably wondering if I like dick. Yes I do. I love some good dick, but that's it, that's all. No relationship, no man trying to run my shit. When I need some good dick I go out and get some! I'm a good looking bitch with money, niggas are all over me, but they're only good for a fuck. I keep a few on the side, who won't disappoint me in bed. Most of the time Spin takes care of business, so I don't have to go anywhere else, but once in a while a woman needs a man's touch down there.

Anyway, my wifeys and I are going to hit the club tonight and recruit. Suhey, Nikki and Destiny have got late night calls, so they're not coming, plus I don't think it will be a good idea for Nikki to meet Spin just yet, or ever, for that matter. I've got plans for the girl, and with Spin in the way it may become impossible.

I pull up at the hotel that Suhey is working from today. I park the car and tell Spin to run up there to get my drop from Suhey for me. She gets out looking sexy as hell, smiling at me from ear to ear for no damn reason. She blows me kisses and shit. I do the same, just to keep her happy. As soon as she's out of earshot, I call Suhey at the room hoping she will pick up before Spin gets up there. Thank God she did.

"Hey Suhey, this is Vanilla, Spin is on her way up to get my drop. I will come and see you tomorrow, I miss that fine ass." She giggles, and agrees with me of course.

"Alright V, Spin is knocking at the door now, so I'll see you tomorrow, Ma."

"Alright baby, until then."

I hang up the phone, and about three minutes later watch Spin come down the stairs on her way back to the car. The closer she gets to the car the more I see the frown on her face. So when she gets in the car and slams my damn door, I snap on her crazy ass.

"What the hell is wrong with you? You got out the car smiling and shit, you get back in looking like someone killed your mama! And don't slam my fucking door like that ever again! You got something to say, say it." So she comes up with this crazy shit!

"Did you fuck her?" She asks me, serious as hell.

So I snap back at her, "What the hell did you say, Spin?" I look at her, shocked; I can't believe she thinks she can question me! "Spin, where the hell did you come up with that?"

So she gives me a dumb ass answer.

"Well, I walk up to the door, the bitch is smiling from ear to ear, and I know you just got off the phone with her; I heard her through the door. So are you going to see her tomorrow, huh?"

"Listen, Spin, I've got to see her tomorrow but not for the reason you think. And don't ask me crazy shit like that! If I wanted to fuck that hoe I would have done it by now!"

"You probably did, Vanilla!" She starts crying, looking out the window.

"You know what, Spin; just shut the fuck up talking to me alright!"

"Whatever, V."

I turn up the radio, bump the music as loud as I can, and ignore the crazy bitch as I pull out of the parking lot, mad as hell. I decide Trina is not going to calm me down, so I put a little 2pac in and bump *Changes*. She still doesn't say a word until we get to the other room in Southfield and pick up the drop from Destiny. I'll get Nikki's tomorrow; I won't even dare to go there with this crazy bitch.

Sophia and Diamond are meeting us at their condo. I hate driving through Dearborn - too many police - but that's where their condo is; Fairlane Town Centre. $3,000 a month! *My* house is not even that much. I try to tell them that they are better off buying a house, but do they listen? Hell no! Fuck it, it's their money. If they've got it, spend it.

I have a house in Novi; a suburb in the D area. Spin is the only one who knows where I live. Well, her and my best friend, and, of course, my family. That's my getaway spot.

Spin puts her hand on my thigh; smirks with those sexy lips and puts her head on my shoulder. I laugh at her; tell her I love her, and that I'm sorry for yelling at her. I also tell her to stop tripping and questioning me. She nods her head.

We pull up at the apartment. I call the girls and tell them we are outside.

"It's 10.30 pm! Come the hell on, the club is off the hook by now!"

Twenty minutes later they finally come down, apologizing before even getting in the car. I just shake my head and pull out.

Sophie hands me a CD she brought with her. Rock Bottom, they're Detroit cats. She tells me what track to put it on. It's our song, *Gatored up*. You've got to own a pair of gator shoes if you're anybody in the D. We bump it loud as hell.

We finally pull up at the club at 11.40pm, valet park, and get out looking ghetto fabulous. We get special treatment; the valet guy knows me very well, so does the doorman, the bartender, the waitress, the manager and the owner. Yeah, it's good! I slip the valet guy $50 and tell him thank you. Spin holds my hand; she always wants people to know she's with me every chance she gets. Sophia holds my other arm. Diamond is next to Spin.

Like always I get much love at the door. I never get searched, so Spin always packs the little .22 in her purse. People are spiteful, so I've got to watch my back.

Emilia Szleszynska

Spin screams over the music, "What do you want to drink?"

I say, "Get me two bottles of Rose Moet, a double shot of Henny - one ice, a bottle of Crissy, and whatever else you want."

They laugh, and Sophia says, "Hell, do we need anything else? We're going to be drunk as hell."

So I tell her, "You may be, you know I kill two bottles to the head." They laugh again.

We sit in the VIP section, and because we took so long, the waitress has spotted us. Her name is "Legs"; a fine older sister. She smiles with all her pretty teeth and asks how many bottles we want. I give her our order and tell her to hook me up on the Henny. She says she's got me. About five minutes later, our drinks show up while the DJ is playing *Shake Ya Ass* by Mystikal.

Sophia's ass is dancing already, looking for some hoes to dance with. Spin is doing her job, leaving business cards and flyers in the bathroom; at the front door; in the women's dressing room; on tables. She comes back with a sexy dancer named "Strawberry", who asks me if I want a dance.

I politely decline and tell her to dance for Diamond, who looks like she wants to fuck the girl right there and then. If she could she would, I know that for sure. The girl smiles and says ok. Now it's time to relax.

I'm eyeing this sexy ass dude standing by himself. He's been glancing over here too. Spin peeps it; moves closer to me and kisses my cheek. I look over at him. He shakes his head and laughs. I smile back and tell Spin to go over there and give him a business card. She frowns, but does what I say. He reads it, smiles, and comes over to our table to introduce himself. He says his name is "Pops", then he takes my hand and kisses it – up close, he's not really 'all that'. He looks like a little thug and that makes him sexy. So does all the bling bling he has on.

I introduce my girls to him. He knows the dancer, Strawberry. I'm not surprised. Spin isn't smiling anymore. I tell him she is my wife;

that makes her happy. He stares hard and smiles. He doesn't seem surprised.

Finally he says, "I would ask you ladies if you would like something to drink, but it looks like you are set for the night."

I smile and say, "Yes, we are thank you."

He asks, "Is it OK if I call you and take you out some time? You and your wife, I mean." I look at Spin.

She says, "I don't care, it's up to you, Ma." I tell him to give me a call; we can talk about it.

It's somebody's birthday, whose I don't know. I look around and see my boy, Fresh, and couple of his boys. He sees me and waves me over. I grab my bottle of Crissy, and tell Spin I'll be right back, I'm going to find somebody to dance for her. She's tipsy, so she doesn't care.

Fresh tells me it's his boy Chill's birthday. Chill is a cat from the hood that we grew up with. I signal for Legs; tell her to get my man a bottle and whatever he wants. I look back; see Pops is watching me; talking to Legs. I kick it with my homies for a minute then go halla at the Manager and the owner. By the time I get back to the table, I see all three of my girls, tipsy as hell, with sexy women all over them. Spin jumps up and tries to hug me. I tell her to sit down and enjoy herself. I'm cool. She does as I say, like always.

I look around the club and see Pops is about to leave – it's 1.15am. He stops by the table and says goodnight. He kisses my hand again, and then does the same with Spin. I can see she likes him. Thank God, because I was going to see him one way or another.

I finally decide to get a dance from this girl named Simone. My girls and me switch dancers. Then, the lights come on and it's time to get the hell out. I don't leave until everybody else is gone. I pay the door man to walk us back to the car, just in case some broke ass dude tries to hit a lick. Well it's not going to be me. I work too hard for my money. I pay the dancers about $600 for some ass shaking, all the pussy I get, and all those women I got. But all this is nothing but a big-ass show. It's about who's got more money than who.

I call Legs over; ask her what my bill is. She smiles and says that Pops took care of it, and the tip. I smile, not really surprised. I knew I liked something about him. I ask her how much it was, and she says $720. I give her a $100 tip. She shows me all those pretty teeth and says, "Thank you, drive safe," hugs me and the girls and tells me to come back soon. She knows I will.

My mind is still on Pops; he got some Brownie points for that. He definitely got some brownie points. I tell Spin about him picking up the bill on our way out the door. She smiles and says, "That's an Iceberg dress you can buy me tomorrow, then. I saw one I really like at *Rags*."

I tell her to shut up. She cracks up. We finally walk out the door and get in the car. I put in Destiny's Child; *Survivor*. I try to sing it, if that's what you want to call it, as I pull out the parking lot banging and waving to Fresh, Chill, and all my other homies from the hood.

We take the long way home down seven Mile, East to the West side. We go to Sophia's and Diamond's Condo in Dearborn for the night. There are only a few cars on the E-way, so we get there pretty fast.

I tell the girls about getting Simone's number, they laugh. I think to myself, I've finally got my seventh hoe. Mission accomplished. Ha-ha.

My BB goes off. I don't touch it, because I don't want Spin to look at it. I look over at her. She's knocked out. I look at my BB; it's Nikki.

It says "I miss you. Hope to see you tomorrow."

I smile. I tell my girl Sophia to BB her back and tell her I said I miss her too, and I'll be there to take her to lunch tomorrow." I look at Spin while I talk, hoping she is really sleeping because I don't feel like fighting at 3.00am on the E-way. Thank God she is really sleeping.

Sophia asks me about Nikki. I just smile. She shakes her head and laughs. Diamond is knocked out too. I take Destiny's Child out, put in R. Kelly, and ride smooth all the way to Dearborn. Tomorrow is my special day with Nikki. I cannot wait. I can only imagine what it will be like this time, since we're past the first stage. Something tells me it's going to be beautiful, very beautiful. I can't wait.

Chapter 2:

_____

Damn I'm late. It's 12.45pm. Half the day is gone. Nikki has been waiting on me since 11.30am. I couldn't call her till 12.30pm, because Spin was with me, and would have been tripping.

As soon as I leave the Condo I call my new "Star." That's what her name will be, "Star"; that's what comes to my mind when I think of her.

I look ghetto fabulous. I've got on my Gucci Capri pants, a baby pink halter top with baby pink gator sandals to match, and a Congo hat. My Gucci glasses and purse also go with it. I keep a change of clothes in the car whenever I go out, because you never know if you'll be able to make it back home. I don't most of the time. Diamond and Sophia are going back to work around 3pm; one on the West Side, one on the East Side.

Suhey and Destiny are at two different locations. As soon as I pick up "Star", I've got to go and pick up my drop from them, then go to lunch; money first, always.

My phone is ringing off the hook - it's work time again. It's lunch time; some of these men would rather eat pussy on their 30 minute break from the office than food. I guess to them this *is* food.

My phone rings again. I answer and say, "Hi, Mama."

It's my mom; I change my tone of voice. She asks when I'm coming over to see her.

I say, "Probably tomorrow."

I tell her this even though I'm totally unsure. She says I'd better be there, and that I should call my sister. I promise her I will. I ask her about Daddy. She says he's the same; getting on her nerves. We talk for about 10 minutes about my sister's school, my mom's job, my dad's business. My dad owns a car dealership. All my girls cashed their cars out, keeping the money in the family. I'm the only one paying $780 a month for this damn Cadillac, because of my age. My insurance is sky high too, because my driving record is hit. I've got two other used cars I bought from my father; a '96 Impala, and my favourite, a '96 Eldorado. I paid $5,500 to make it a drop top. I've got 15s in all three of my cars; DVDs in both headrests and in the dashboard. The Impala, originally with only 89,000 miles on it, has no 20s, 22s, or 24s, it's just as is! Everywhere I go niggas are trying to buy it. Hell no! That's *my* toy.

My mind goes back to my mom. I finally say, "Love you, bye," and call my sister. She's not home; good, I don't feel like talking right now. I leave her a brief message.

I finally pull up in front of Nikki's hotel. I call her room. She doesn't pick up. I'm getting nervous, then I see the most beautiful woman I have seen in a long time walk out of Room 211, smiling. I hang the phone up. I smile back, get out of the car and open the passenger door for her. She says thank you and gets in. She tells me she likes my car as she plays with the DVD and radio. I don't say anything just yet. She stops and asks me what I want to hear?

I say, "Whatever you want."

She says something that makes me love her on the spot.

"It's your car, your radio, Baby, whatever you want to hear."

I smile from ear to ear; if she only knew what that means to me. I put in Eminem. She says she loves him.

I say, "Yeah, who doesn't in the D?"

We laugh and talk until we get all the way to *Starters*. It's packed, like always. I park in the alley and pray that my Caddy will be there when I come back. Nikki gets out looking as fine as ever. She's got on a Prada dress with matching purse, and the sexiest stilettos I've seen in a while. Her hair is halfway down her back - all real, all hers, I found out yesterday when I was pulling it; while she was between my legs. Sorry, just had to share that with you. Ha-ha.

She has the most beautiful eyes. Green, brown, blue; all of those colors mixed together. The ass is just perfect; she's got J-low beat. She has nice titties, no stomach and no kids; she's only 21. She's still older than me but age is nothing but a number. I feel at least 29, not 19. Life has been hard and easy at the same time. Like they say, pimping isn't easy, but somebody's got to do it. That's what the plate on my Pink Mary Kay Caddy says in black and pink. You've got to love it.

We walk into the restaurant and get a table for two. I look around to see if I see any familiar faces. No-one so far, but it's a big place. I won't be surprised if somebody comes out of nowhere and starts talking me to death. I pray that doesn't happen.

We already know what we want to eat; two surf and turfs, a bottle of Black Label Moet, a double shot of Henny – straight, and a coke on the side - one ice. She order's Remy on Ice. It takes about five minutes for our drinks to get here, 20 for our food. We talk about everything; our families, the past, the present, and the future. In particular though, we talk about our future. We discuss what we can do together, how we're going to make money, how we're going to make things better, etc. I'm loving every moment of it, making plans in my mind for the future.

The waitress comes to check on us. I tell her we're doing okay and ask for a refill on our drinks. I have not enjoyed myself like this in a while. Almost every time I take Spin out she accuses me of looking at somebody or flirting, which is true half the time, but still, who does she think she is checking me in public?

I look over at the bar and can't believe who I see. He must have been there since we came in. Yes, it's Pops, looking sexy with his gator sandals on. He's wearing jean shorts, a wife beater, and those platinum iced-out Cartiers are bling blinging, making every other nigga in here look like a bum. He looks at me, smiles and winks. I do the same.

I call my waitress over and ask if the man over there has paid his bill yet. She looks surprised and tells me, "not yet." I ask her not to tell him until we leave. Nikki is looking confused, I tell her I'll explain later. She smiles and says okay. I pay my bill, and his, which is about $250 plus a tip. Taking Nikki by the hand, I walk out, smiling. When I get to my car I smile harder and thank God it's still there.

I look in front and behind me and say "Shit, were blocked in." I tell Nikki to get in and lock the doors while I go back inside and ask somebody to make an announcement and tell them to move either the Jaguar behind me, which was there when we first got here, or the raggedy ass Ford that looks like it's been needing a paint job for the last 10 years if not more.

Finally, about a minute after they announce it, two brothers come to the door. One of them is Pops. I assume the Jag is his. He tells the other brother that he's about to leave anyway, so he can go back and finish his dinner. He looks at me and smiles.

As we walk out the door, he says, "Thank you for dinner."

"You're welcome. Thank you for the drinks last night." I respond.

He laughs and says, "You have an expensive habit."

So I tell him, "I've always got to have the best in everything."

He looks at my car and says, "Huh, I see."

"Do you mean the car or the woman?" I ask.

"Both." He replies.

We both laugh. He moves the Jaguar up next to me and introduces himself to Nikki, who smiles but doesn't say too much. Just the way I like it. He asks when is a good time to call me so we can hook up. He says my friend can come too; he would love to introduce her to one of his boys. I laugh at that one and tell him in a tone of voice that he knows I mean, "I don't share my women with strangers."

"I was waiting for you to say something like that." He says.

"Why?" I ask.

He just says it's obvious. I leave it at that. I tell him I'll call him soon, and then I remember I've got money to pick up, so I make it short and sweet and watch him pull out in his 2009 black Jaguar.

Nikki laughs and says, "I didn't think you liked men."

I look at her and say, "I don't, but their money is green just like ours."

She smiles and says, "true, true."

She asks if she can put in Rock Bottom. I say go ahead, and we ride out, hit the freeway, and get back to work. We've got to go and get some money. I'm taking her back to the room so she can make some money. Spin is blowing up my BB. I don't answer my cell phone. I know I've got hell coming. I try not to think about it so that my day won't be ruined.

Chapter 3:
_____

I look at my phone; Sophia and Diamond are on their way to their rooms. They dropped Spin off at her room. A few minutes later, Suhey and Destiny call from their room, they're ready to get paid. My phone has been ringing since 12:00pm, but I have not been answering because no-one was where they were supposed to be. Now it's 3:40pm, and it's time to get paid. It's bad enough we missed out on the lunch hour calls.

By 4:10pm I'm finally alone, everybody is where they need to be. My phone is ringing, and Sophia and Destiny have got clients on their way.

Spin is still calling. I won't call back. I have no client to send to her, and once I do, I won't have a choice but to talk to her. In a way I hope no-one will call in that area, because I don't want to hear her mouth. I still love her, but things just aren't the same anymore. And now with Star in the picture, I know there are going to be problems; it's just a matter of time. I'm pulling up at Detroit Free Press, I have to renew my ads for the girls, then go to the bank and make a deposit. The bank is closed now, but as long as I make it to the drop box I'm cool.

I walk in and see the same face behind the counter I've been seeing for the last three years. An older black woman who's never been nice to me or the girls whenever we come up here; probably because she knows what we put the ads in for. Oh well, there's nothing she can do but put them in there as long as I pay. I pay for the next four weeks, so I won't have to come back up here all the time. I only renew my ads on the

Internet when I get new girls. The ones in the Yellow Pages book last all year.

Now, I've got to hit the bank.

"5:45pm? Damn, where'd the day go?" I say out loud while looking at my Rolex; a present from Spin I got for Christmas. A broke down looking pimp named "Sweet James" walks in and tries to halla. I look back and laugh and tell him to make some money rather than halla at me. The nigga can't stand me because at least four of his girls left and came to work for me until they'd got enough money saved up to do what they wanted to do. They know they're always welcome to come back, and some call when they need to make a few bucks. I look out for them, but my girls always come first.

I look at his hoe, she's kind of cute and could be worked on. I hand her a business card. He snaps. She gets mad and starts yelling at him. Obviously I've started some shit and didn't even know it. He tells her to throw the shit out or she's going to get her ass beat. She challenges the nigga and tells him to try it. She tells him she's still trying to figure out why she's with his broke down ass. I like her already.

She looks right at me and says, "Can you give me a ride?"

I look over at Sweet James and he says, "You can have the dumb hoe if you want, I've got enough hoes. I don't need one with a big-ass mouth like that."

She laughs at him and says, "You've got three broke down dirty bitches in one hotel room, and they haven't made a dime in two days! I'm the best thing that ever came your way."

She storms out the door. I go out behind her laughing. Now I can't wait to call Spin and tell her what happened, she's going to love this one.

I say to the girl, "Slow down and relax, it's going to be cool. My car is parked around the corner, you can't miss it."

We go around the loop and my Caddy is still there, thank God! My baby looks like she needs a bath, I'd better hit the car wash right after the bank; I can't be riding around in a dirty ass whip.

She looks surprised and says, "Is this yours?" I just smile.

She's too geeked now. I get in the Caddy and find my 8Ball & MJG and bump *Pimp Hard.* Her ghetto ass is screaming, "This is my shit girl!" I just smile and tell myself I've got some work on my hands. We finally pull off. I tell her my name. She says her name is Ayanna, and this means beautiful flower. I think in my mind that once I'm done with her, she will be a beautiful flower, *my* beautiful flower.

A call comes in for Spin. Once I leave the bank, I finally call her. I tell her my phone has been tripping. She knows I'm lying but doesn't say shit. I tell her I've got somebody I want her to meet and take shopping. I tell her about Sweet James and what happened; this makes her day. She says she'll be ready to bounce once she's finished this client. I get a few calls for each of the girls; they're booked 'til at least 1:00am. No clubbing tonight.

I pick up Spin and hit the mall to get "Flower" some hook-ups while it's still open. Meanwhile she gets her nails and toes done. Spin's going to hook up her hair in the room. She can hook up some shit with some hair and glue. We get a few packs of 100% human hair from the Beauty Supply store at the mall, as well as some glue and whatever else she needs. Two hours later, and $1,500 in the hole, we are kicked out of the mall at 9:15pm. My new girl is happier than ever before; she can't wait to put her new clothes on and get her hair done.

My phone rings, it's a number I don't recognize. I pick up and say, "Vanilla's Ladies."

A sweet female voice comes over the phone, "Hello, may I speak to Vanilla please?"

I ask who is calling. She says, "It's Simone, the girl from *007.*"

I smile and say "What up doe Boo?"

She wants to know if she can she work, and what time can she start. I smile really hard, look over at Spin and make sure she hears me.

"You want to start work now?" Spin smiles and shakes her head. So does Flower, with her ghetto ass. I ask Simone where she's at. She says she's on Fenkell and Evergreen, across the street from the Mobil; second house on the corner. I tell her I'll be there in 15 minutes to take her to the room; Spin's room.

I'm happy as hell today, all my girls are booked for the whole night, and I just swooped two hoes in one day! Oh boy!

 I take 8Ball and MJG out and put in the Street Lordz. Ayanna claims she's fucked Fat Mike. I laugh and say, "Who hasn't?" We all laugh and just jam to the music. Life is good!

Finally we pick Simone up, and we're on our way to the room. Twenty minutes later we finally get there. I tell Spin to go and get another room for herself and use the room she was already in for work only. I tell her not to let the girls know where the other room is. I don't trust them just yet. Once I know they're down to do the damn thing I will feel more comfortable; once they've done a few clients. Spin does what I say, then gives the girls her cell phone number and tells them to call if they need anything once she leaves; after she's finished doing Ayanna's hair. I kick it with them for a minute, and then me and Spin go to her new room.

I've got to get away somehow, although I have not figured that part out yet. I promised Suhey I'd see her tonight; she's blowing me up. My BB is on vibrate so Spin can't hear it. I go to the bathroom and BB Suhey back, telling her I will be there in an hour or two because Spin is tripping. I also tell her to stop calling me so damn much!

I get out of the bathroom and the first thing that comes out of Spin's mouth is: "where we going tonight?" It's Friday night.

I look at her and say "No damn where."

She frowns and says "Why? It's Friday!"

I say "Because I'm going to my sister's house for the night. I want to see my nephew and I'm going to spend the day with my mama and the family tomorrow, so I want to be close by there."

She says, "Yeah right."

I look at her like she's crazy, and snap, "Bitch, I don't have to lie to you about my family!"

She says, "I'm sorry; I didn't mean to say it like that."

I'm so glad she said something stupid, so I can use that as an excuse to leave. I grab my purse and hit the door. She blocks me, with tears in her eyes. I hate this shit!

"Please baby, don't leave here being mad at me."

I look at her seriously and say, "I'm not mad yet, but I will be if you don't get out my way and let me do what I've got to do."

She looks hurt and scared, but she moves over slowly. I open the door and slam it behind me, then call her cell phone. She picks up, crying.

I say, "Make sure you do ghetto girl's hair tonight."

She says okay and tells me she loves me, I say I love her too and I tell her to stop acting stupid.

Finally I'm alone! I really, really like being alone sometimes. Being around all these women all day makes you go crazy!

I just sit there in my car for about five minutes while I call Suhey and tell her I'm on my way. Finally I leave the parking lot of the hotel. I used to think Suhey was going to take Spin's spot, but she's too immature and she's not all that street smart. If I let her go, she won't know what to do with herself. She needs somebody to tell her what to do, when to do it, and how to do it. And I love being the one to do that.

I met her at this club called *Pretty Women* on East Seven Mile and Van Dyke, in Detroit. A little hole in the wall place, but cool to go and chill out at. She was on stage, dancing, and I came up to tip her. Once she'd seen the $50 I'd put in her g-string she moved it and let me see her fat, hot, wet, ready-to-fuck pussy. When it was time for her to get off stage, she came over to my table and introduced herself. She's beautiful as hell, the hair, the skin, just the way I like it. Damn, I never will forget that day.

Back to reality. I finally pull up at the hotel at about 10:45pm. Her next client isn't coming until 1:00am, and that's her last client for the night. I park, lock the car, call her room, and tell her I'm on my way up. She stands at the door smiling, waiting for me to come up the stairs. I walk into her room, closing the door behind me. I give her a hug, and kiss those sexy lips. She looks beautiful with just the towel on. I want to pull it off and throw her on the bed and fuck the shit out of her, like I did the night we met.

Business first. She gives me my $1,100 drop. I put the money up, and we talk about her crazy clients. I tell her about what happened with Sweet James and about Ayanna's ghetto ass and the new girl, Simone. I don't even mention Nikki. She asks why Spin was looking all pissed off last night; I look at her and tell her, "You know the girl is crazy; she always thinks I'm doing something wrong."

She laughs and says, "she's not lying."

I laugh and tell her to shut up. She tells me about one of her perverted clients, an old white man who loves nasty shit. He gave her $1000 to shit in his mouth! That shit makes me want to puke, but it seems to be a normal thing that these clients request when they call. It's a damn shame to pay money to get shit on. But they like it, so I love it!

My phone rings; I don't recognize the number, so I change my voice when I answer. I don't say my usual "Vanilla's Ladies", just a weak, "Hello?"

A sexy, familiar male voice comes over the phone and says, "May I speak to Vanilla please?"

I don't want to say this is me because it might be the Police.

So I ask, "Who's calling?"

He answers, "Pops."

I smile and say, "This is Vanilla, how are you doing?"

He responds and we talk for a while. He wants me to meet him at the Renaissance Center, Room 412. He says he has a surprise for me. I don't tell Suhey that because I don't want her to think I'm dissing her for some dick. I go to the bathroom and pretend it was a family matter. She's dizzy enough to go for it. Spin would have thrown a fit. That reminds me, I've got to call her.

I apologize to Suhey and tell her I will make it up to her, but I have to take care of this. She says she understands and she wishes I could stay. She says she's horny as hell. I tell her that Destiny is done for the night and, if she wants, I can call her and tell her to come down and take care of her. She smiles and kisses me, which tells me that will do it. I hug her and leave her. One part of me wants to stay and fuck the shit out of her, but the other part wants to see what Pops is about. I go with the other part since I know what the first part is like already.

Chapter 4:

It only takes me 10 minutes to get to the Renaissance Centre since I was already in downtown Detroit. I valet park and go into the lobby. I call him back on the number he called me from, but, as I'm dialing the number, I see him sitting on the couch in the lobby just watching me, smiling. I hang the phone up and walk over to the elevator, he follows me. We get in together. I don't say much, just a weak, "Hello". He laughs and shakes his head. We get off the elevator and I follow him to his room.

He opens the door. The lights are dimmed, slow jazz is playing, candles are lit, and there are flowers (white roses) on the bed, table, chair, on top of the T.V., in the bathtub - everywhere. There is a bottle of Crissy and two champagne glasses. I also spot a bottle of Black Label Moet, a pint of Hennessey and a bottle of Coke. All of my favorite drinks. He gets more brownie points for a good memory. I laugh. He tells me to make myself comfortable, while he pops the Crissy bottle. I tell him he didn't have to go out of his way for me, but he says, "Trust me, I didn't."

Well excuse me then! I think in my mind. He pours the champagne in the glasses and brings one to me. We make a toast for the future and take a sip. He tells me I look beautiful today. I laugh and say, "Yeah right, I've been running around for the last two days like a chicken with its head cut off, dealing with crazy people! I think I'm just going to quit and get a nine to five."

He laughs and looks really relaxed.

He responds, "Nine to five doesn't buy Gucci, Prada, and Gators."

"You ain't lying; maybe I'll just find a man to do all that then, are you volunteering?"

"Shit, to keep it real with you baby girl, that's why I don't have a woman. Women these days ain't on my level, they ain't even got a nine to five or a hustle, but they're always pulling their hand out, talking about gimmie, gimmie gimmie! I don't mind giving to a woman who's got her shit together, because when I might need her, she going to be there for a nigga."

I nod my head, and let him continue talking.

"Plus I've got too much to offer than to settle down with just anybody."

I ask a question now.

"What made you pay for my drinks then? You didn't know anything about me, or, did you?"

"Well, I didn't, but then I asked Tony (the owner of the club) if he knew anything about you and your girls. He told me you were the one I needed to halla at, not your girls. To be honest with you, at first I just thought you were some dancers on their day off at the club until your girl gave me your business card."

I just smile at him and make sure I clear the air.

"Just so you know, I don't get down like that. My girls do their thing; I put shit together. I may be a lesbian, but I'm no hoe."

He laughs and excuses himself while his phone rings. He goes into the bathroom. I hear something about 70 Gs…45 minutes…Jefferson… he'd be there. Then Pops comes back out of the bathroom and asks me if I would mind making a run with him. He explains that he didn't know this was going to happen, but he can't put it off. I tell him I understand and say, "Let's roll."

He smiles, walks up to me and kisses me on my forehead. I feel like a little child. We walk out after he grabs his briefcase. I tell him I'll drive.

"Cool, let's do this." He says.

We go downstairs quietly. I approach the valet guy and give him my ticket. They pull the caddy up. We get in and roll out.

Pops says, "If I ever drove this car, niggas would know it wasn't my shit. It's a woman's ride; it's bright is hell!"

"That's why I like it, pink is my favorite color! Where are we going?" I ask.

"We're going to the Big Boy on Jefferson."

I say cool and put in Trina. He puts his hand around my seat, looks over and smiles. I smile back.

Five minutes later we're at the Big Boy. Pops tells me to pull up next to the Land Rover truck. I do. I reach into my purse and put my 45 on my lap. Pops looks surprised and nervous. I hide it between my thighs with my hand still on the trigger and smile.

"It's for protection only. I don't know you that well and I don't know who you're dealing with in the truck." I explain.

He looks nervous but gets out the car, grabs the briefcase and gets in the Rover. I keep my eye on everything that's going on. The nigga driving the Rover looks through his window at me, all paranoid and shit. Then he pulls off like he's crazy; tires squeaking and dust flying.

I didn't put the car in 'park', I was just holding the brake pad while it was in 'drive'. So I let go, hit the gas and I'm right on his ass, wishing I was in the Impala so that the nigga wouldn't even have a chance. He really doesn't have much of a chance to lose me in the caddy, but he's really trying to get away from me. Why, I have no fucking clue, but I will find out. I'm dialing Pops' phone. No answer. I keep hitting redial. Someone else answers; it's the ol' boy that's driving.

"Bitch, are you the Police?"

"Hell no, I ain't the damn Police! What the hell are you doing with my nigga? You've got me burning rubber on the middle of Jefferson and shit! The Police *will* be on our ass if you don't stop!"

"Hell no! As far as I know you're the Po-Po, bitch. You must be crazy if you think I'm going to stop!"

I laugh out of anger and tell him, "My gas tank is on max; we can do this until one of us runs out of gas, or until you let my boy out the car!" I'm screaming all this on the speaker phone.

He hangs up and still tries to lose me. I keep calling back - no answer. I'm pissed off now. That fool asked for it; I hit his shit with the caddy. Fuck it, I've got insurance and two more cars to drive. He calls me back not even a minute later.

I pick up and say, "Are you ready to stop? Next time I'm shooting at your ass! Put my boy on the phone so I know he's alright."

He says "No, bitch."

I scream on the phone, "Put Pops on the phone or your shit is going to get shut up; try me if you want to!"

I fire a blank in the air out the window while he's trying to lose me on the side streets. It's about 12:00am; the Police are probably everywhere, but I'm so mad I really don't give a fuck!

He screams and says, "Bitch, you're crazy!"

I tell him, "You ain't seen crazy yet."

Pops gets on the phone.

"Vanilla?" He says.

I ask him, "Does he have a gun?"

"No." He replies.

I hang up, look out the window, and shoot the left back tire of his truck. Then I shoot the back window. He's screaming through the phone when I call back; I can't understand what he's saying.

"Let's try this one more time." I say.

He finally pulls over. I pull up next to him, jump out of the car, run up to the truck, break the driver side window, and point the 45 straight at his temple. He looks like a scary ass bitch. I still can't believe this fool had no gun! He begs me not to shoot him.

Pops jumps out of the truck and walks round to my side with two briefcases in his hands; one of them, the same one we left the hotel with. He sees the anger in my eyes and says, "Baby girl, don't do it, the nigga ain't worth it." He knocks out the guy's grill with one blow, drags him out the car and whoops his ass like there is no tomorrow.

I get in the truck; grab his car keys, cell-phone, and even the face off his radio. Hell, I even take his C.D. case. I get out and make my way back to my car. Pops throws him behind the wheel of the truck and jumps in the caddy.

I pull off, rubber burning. He starts laughing. I look at him like he's crazy and say "What the fuck is so funny?"

"You are, you crazy dog." He says

I start laughing; I can't help it anymore more. He tells me to pull over. I ask why, still holding the 45 in my hand. He bends down to get the briefcase. He opens one of the briefcases and throws a money clip on my lap with $25,000 in it, at least that's what the sticker says and from the look of it, all of it is there. I look at him and say, "What's this for?"

He says, "For keeping it real."

I finally pull over. He leans in and kisses me with so much passion I forget I don't like men; shit, I forget he's a man! I've never felt like this before; never let a man kiss me with this much passion; never enjoyed a kiss like this. Finally, after what it seems like eternity, he pulls away, kisses my forehead, then I pull out and drive back towards the room. We don't say anything until we get in the room.

He grabs me, picks me up, throws me on the bed and starts kissing me so hard and deep, on my lips, my nose, eyes, ears, and neck. Slowly, he kisses my chest, removing my halter top. I finally come back to my senses and push him away. What the hell am I thinking? I'm about to have sex with a man, the thought of it scares me, not because of the sex, but because I'm really feeling this cat.

I get up, put my shirt back on, walk over to the table and crack open the Hennessey. I don't even bother to mix it with coke; I just put an ice cube in the glass and drink it straight. I make him a drink and pass it to him. He takes it and tells me to sit down on the bed and relax. He says I don't have to do anything I don't want to do. I look at him and say I know that. Then I grab the phone and go to the bathroom.

I call Spin. I make it short and sweet. She says Simone had three clients and Ayanna had four. I transfer my calls to her cell-phone so that she can book the calls for the night. I act like I'm at my sister's house. I tell her I love her and miss her and I really mean it, then I hang up.

I'm about to walk out when I remember to call Destiny. I tell her to go and see Suhey right away and take care of her for me. She laughs and says she'll do it with pleasure.

"Yeah, I bet you will. I reply.

I hang up and finally walk out the bathroom. I pop open the Moet bottle and mix a drink with my Hennessey. I make one for Pops as well. He asks if I'm alright. I just nod and lay my head on his lap. He rubs my hair with his hand and tells me he would do anything for me. He knows I've got his back and he wants me to know he's got mine.

We talk about what happened. He tells me he knows he's got shit on his hands, because he took that ol' boy's shit and he doesn't want any beef. He says he's got to get shit straight with the big man in charge about the ol' boy that we fucked up tonight, he's going to give the boss man his shit back, and only wants to deal with him directly from now on.

Pops picks up his phone, lies back and calls the main man in charge to sort shit out. He puts him in check like *he's* the one who took *his* shit. From what I understand, ol' boy's got some more drama coming his way from his own people. The big man tells Pops to keep whatever he's got; he deserves it for the hassle we went through, and he tells him he's got a down-ass chick. Pops smiles, kisses me and says, "Yeah, I know, that's my 'ride and die' chick." I smile at him and kiss his hand.

He hangs up. We talk more about what happened and about ourselves: family, future, past and anything else we can think of. Before we know it, it's 4:30am and he asks me if I want to take a nap. I say no, and tell him something I can't believe is coming out of my mouth.

"I don't want a nap; I want you to make love to me."

Maybe it's the Henny talking. Pops looks at me, confused, and says, "What did you just say?"

"You heard me. Or didn't you?" I ask.

"Yeah, I thought I heard you, but I want to make sure that's what I heard."

"I said I want you to make love to me and I mean just that. I don't want us to have sex or fuck; I want us to make love. Can you do that?"

He smiles, walks over to me while I'm making another drink and picks me up (still with the drink in my hand) sits me on the bed, kisses my forehead, my nose, my lips, my whole face.

I finally put the drink down after taking a sip and giving him a sip. I lay down across the king size bed while jazz is playing in the air. The lights are dimmed and I enjoy his sexy lips on my body. He looks at me one more time and says, "Are you sure you want to do this?"

"If you ask me one more time I will change my mind." I tell him.

"Trust me; I ain't going to ask again!"

We laugh while he kisses me softly. My lips press against his, my tongue mixes with his, tasting the liquor on his breath, which tastes really sweet right about now. I have a nice buzz going on; so does he. I really feel this will be a good morning. He takes my halter top off once again and looks at me with questioning eyes. I just laugh and throw it on the love seat, letting him know he doesn't have to worry about me putting it back on this time.

He relaxes and tells me to turn over and lie on my stomach. I look at him funny, but I do it. I close my eyes and relax. He slowly takes my pants and my shoes off leaving only the G-string on. He tells me I look so beautiful. It doesn't make any sense, he can't get over how big my ass is compared to the rest of my body. Not to brag, but I'm very happy with my body, God has really blessed me.

He starts rubbing my feet, taking his time. He goes up to my calves, my thighs and finally my fat ass; he really takes his time there. He massages me from head to toe for about an hour. I feel so relaxed and turned on. I'm ready to make love to him.

It's almost daylight outside. He walks over and closes the blinds; the dim lights stay on. He turns me over and slowly takes my G-string off with his teeth. My whole body is shivering right now. He kisses me again for a long time while his hands are all over me. He rubs my clit with his fingers and tells me how wet I am and that he loves it like that. Then he licks his fingers. He is driving me crazy! I'm loving every minute of it. He teases every part of my body before and I know it, I climax just from him kissing and touching me.

Slowly he starts to kiss my thighs, while he slides his fingers into my wet pussy. He takes them out and licks them, then does the alphabet with his tongue on my clit, driving me crazy. I have never felt anything like this before. He makes me have multiple orgasms. My body experiences things I didn't know it could experience, and the thought of having sex with this man scares me because I just know it's going to be twice as good.

Every time I try to touch him he moves my hands and tells me to let *him* please *me* tonight. I do as he asks, until I can't help it any more. He tries to put my hands down, but I don't let him this time; I make him lay down on the bed. He finally gives in and let me take the rest of his clothes off.

I kiss him. I start from the top of his head and move down to his chest, then finally grab his manhood and kiss the tip of it. I'm a little scared. I tell him I've never done this before.

"You've never had sex with a man before?" He asks.

I laugh while I stroke his 10½ inch, thick-ass dick and say, "No, I've had sex, I've just never sucked any dick, but with you I want to do it." He tells me I don't have to, but I keep kissing it then finally, I put the head in my mouth, ignoring him. I don't want him to change my mind. I really want to do this.

Slowly I move the head in and out my mouth, not using my hands anymore. Each time I move it in and out I go deeper. I look up at him while I'm doing it and see his eyes rolling back; this turns me on even more. I start sucking his dick faster and harder. I get so horny just sucking his dick I start playing with my pussy, I don't think I ever been this horny and wet before. I start thinking about Nikki and Spin; my pussy cums just from that.

He realizes I'm cumming, lies me down on my stomach, lifts my ass up and slowly puts his fat dick into my hot pussy, stroking me slowly while I'm cumming on his dick.

He starts fucking me faster and faster, it hurts but it feels so good, he wants me to ride him. I do as he says. I sit on "my" dick and fuck him like he's never been fucked before. My pussy is so wet you can hear it. He flips me over, fucks me from the side, back, front, standing up, until he's ready to bust a nut. I feel him shaking. I tell him to pull out and cum in my mouth, he does as I say. I swallow all of it and kiss his dick when I'm finish.

We both just lay there holding each other. I look at the clock, it's 7:36am. I tell him we need some sleep; I've got a long day ahead of me. I go and take a shower, brush my teeth and come back to bed. I kiss him then he goes and takes his shower. When he comes back, he lies next to me. We set the alarm for 12:00pm, which gives us four hours to get some sleep.

Chapter 5:

Before I know it, it's 12:00pm and check out time. We get up slowly, looking at each other like we want to make love again, but we both know we don't have time, so we get our shit together and leave.

We kiss in the elevator and give the valet guy our tickets. My caddy pulls up first with a few scratches on the bumper. I look at it and shake my head. I get in. Pops sticks his head in my window, kisses me again and tells me where to go to get my bumper fixed. He says his people will take care of me and he's going to pay for it. I won't argue with that. I tell him I'll do it on Monday; I'll drive the Impala until then.

My phone is ringing like crazy; Spin, Nikki, Suhey, my sister, and my mom have been blowing me up all night and all morning. Pops looks at my phone and says, "You'd better get that." I smile, give him one more kiss, then pull off.

I answer my phone; it's Spin.

"What the fuck are you doing? I've been calling you for hours thinking something had happened and shit."

I laugh and say, "I'm cool; I just had a busy morning and a little accident."

I tell her to keep the phone transfer because I'm going to my mother's house. I'll call her when I get there. I tell her I love her and I miss her.

I call Suhey back see what's up. She tells me about how much fun she had with Destiny, who is still sleeping. I tell her to make her ass get up and go back to the room because I've got calls for her. She's cool with that, so we hang up.

I call Nikki, Sophia and Diamond and get them situated. I tell them about Ayanna and Simone. They are geeked for me. I hang up and finally call my mother to tell her I'm on my way. She says she wants to go shopping. I say, "cool" and tell her I'll be there in 20 minutes. I go to Novi, jump in the Impala and roll to my mother's house in W Bloomfield.

At 1:45pm I'm there, beeping the horn, waiting for her to come out. Eventually she does.

We hit Fair Lane. I buy her, my daddy, my sister and my nephew something each; I can't leave anyone out. My mama asks me where I get all this money from. I tell her I get it from my new boyfriend. She wants to know why she never meets any of them. I tell her it's because they're nobody special and they never last. She tells me I might actually keep one if I stop chasing them away with my big mouth and my 'I don't need a man' attitude. I just laugh.

We drive back, and I pull in in-front of her house. She tells me to come in and eat. I tell her I've got a date.

"He can wait." She says, and gives me the 'what's more important than your mother' speech.

So I go in and eat in record time. I tell her I'll be back tomorrow to go to church with her and daddy, and also to see my sister and my nephew. I kiss my mama and daddy; he just woke up, on his way to work.

I jump in the Impala and hit the streets. It's 5:30pm; hustle time. I call Spin; she had three calls, Ayanna had two and Simone had four. They're killing it. I love it! I tell Spin to take Simone to a different location, and then go back to her room. I'll be over there by 8:00pm.

I'm on my way to go and see Nikki. I call her. She had three calls booked through Spin. I made sure I told her not to have a conversation with Spin, and just to keep it business. She mustn't have said anything because Spin didn't trip.

I call Sophia, Destiny and Diamond; they each had two calls. I'm getting paid today, baby! It seems like my money has doubled since I met Pops. I get a free 25Gs for keeping it real, even though I risked my ass by getting caught up in an armed robbery, a dope case and a whole bunch of other crazy shit. Thank God for being there with me; why he keeps me safe I have no idea, but I'm glad he does what he does. Not only that, but my girls have been getting booked like crazy left and right; making G's daily! I haven't had to lift a hand and I've got $7,500 waiting on me from two days of work. I love it baby! Usually $2,000 a day is cool, but my shit has doubled, even tripled, since Pops came into the picture.

My phone rings, I lose my train of thought. It's my mom; she must have found the $10,000 I left in her bedroom. She asks me where I got it, and if I did something illegal.

"No, just enjoy it." I tell her.

She's cool with that. She's crazy, but you've got to love her, that's just Mama.

Finally, at 6:00pm, I pull up in front of Nikki's hotel. I call her and tell her to come out. She arrives about five minutes later. Damn she looks good! My baby's got on a sporty Coogi dress, fitting perfectly on those curves. Her hair is up in a bun and she's looking at me through gold Versace frames, like a sexy school teacher. Damn I'm lucky. Cats will hate it when they see us together and try to halla and can't get any play. My new baby claims me to the fullest. If you're not spending Gs, she won't even look at you.

She gets in the car, speed talking about everything, then she kisses me and asks me if she can listen to Maya.

"I don't care." I say.

I ask her where she wants to go. She tells me we can go back upstairs if I want. I laugh and say, "I would, but it's that time of the month". It's a lie, of course. After Pops last night I can't even think about having sex anymore; I don't think I can cum anymore! I don't say that out loud though. Honestly, the only person I can even think about having sex with is Pops. I tell myself I've got to get him out my mind for now and concentrate on Nikki.

I tell her to be quiet for a second while I call Spin and tell her Nikki is gone for the day. She does as I say. Spin picks up.

"*Vanilla's Ladies.*"

"Hey baby girl, it's me, take Nikki off, she's done for the day."

"Why?" she asks.

"I don't know, she said she needs a few hours off, so I said cool. You don't want to chase her away already, do you?" She laughs and says cool.

I hang up and look at Nikki. She looks like she wants to ask a question, but she doesn't. Good. I don't feel like explaining anything right now.

"Do you want to go to the movies?" I finally ask her.

"Sure," she says.

So we hit the liquor store. We get a pint of Henny, some ice, some coke, two cups, a bottle of Moet, some junk food, Newports, gum, and water. Everything we need.

We hit the drive-in in South-West Detroit; it's about 7:00pm. We're about to go and see some movie she picked; I can't even remember the name. I park, get comfortable, then excuse myself and go to the bathroom to call Spin. But as I walk over, guess who I see coming out of the men's bathroom. Mr Pops himself! He smiles and tries to hug me. I pull back and tell him he'd better get back to his date. He laughs and tells me to stop tripping and give him a hug. I keep on walking. He grabs my arm and tries to talk to me.

"Crystal, please listen to me for a minute."

I look at him in shock.

"How the fuck do you know my name?" I demand.

He laughs and says, "I know more than you think."

I tell him, "Don't ever use my name in public or in front of anybody again, do you hear me? Do you understand the words coming out of my mouth?"

He looks surprised, and I'm sure he sees that I'm angry, but he just holds me and says, "What's wrong baby, why are you so angry? Is it because I came to the show with somebody; you ain't got time for me? I'm sure *you* ain't here by yourself! I bet you've got at least one of your girls with you, or is it your wifey?"

I just look at him confused while he hits me with the truth, and it hurts. He keeps on and on talking about how I've got a nerve to get mad at him for what he does. I tell him I'm not mad, I just don't like to be used.

He laughs and says, "Baby, nobody used you, I loved making love to you, but after it was over you acted like all you wanted from me was some dick! You haven't called a nigga, or anything. I ain't one of your hoes; I'm not going to chase you, baby girl. I ain't got a woman; all the broads I fuck with ain't anybody. All they want is my money; they don't want a nigga for real. I thought you did, but you prefer pussy over dick, so what the fuck do you want me to do? I want us to be more than fuck partners. You showed me you're real as hell, but until I know it's just me and you, don't expect me not to do what I do."

"Pops, are you alright?" Some light-skinned sister asks him, staring me down all hard and shit.

"Yeah, I'm tight, go back to the truck, this is my peoples here."

"Why are you explaining yourself to this white bitch?!" She asks.

I look at the hoe like she's crazy!

"You don't know shit about me you half-breed bitch." I tell her.

I put the 45 to her head. She freezes.

Pops jumps back and screams, "V, please put the gun down, she ain't worth it, baby."

Half-breed still isn't saying a word.

I look at Pops and say, "Why is it that every time I'm with you I've got to pull out my gun?! You'd better put your hoe in check and make the bitch apologize to me. I'll die before I let a hoe disrespect me!"

He looks at his bitch and says, "Apologize if you want to walk, and trust me she will shoot!"

She looks even more scared and says, "I…I'm sorry."

"Get on your knees and apologize, bitch."

She hesitates.

"I said get on your knees and apologize!"

She does. By then we've got an audience. I see Nikki come my way to see why all the people are around the bathroom. I wave my gun and tell her to go pull the car up. She runs back and does what I say. Thank God I don't have a plate on the outside of the car, just in the window. I get in the car, pull the plate out the window, and tell Nikki to get into the passenger's seat.

I pull off because I'm sure somebody will have called the Police. I hit Ford Road and throw the gun in a ditch after I wipe it clean, just in case they pull us over. I call my mama and tell her that if anybody calls, the Police or anybody, I've been there since 6:30pm with Nikki. It takes me about 10 minutes to get to my mama's house.

I sit on the back porch, angry as hell. Not at the half breed, not about the situation, but about the fact that I'm falling in love with Pops.

Chapter 6:

Pops has been calling my phone since we left the drive-in. I won't answer. Spin has been blowing up my BB too, wanting to know when I'm coming to see her and pick up my drops. She tells me to answer my damn phone! I BB her back and tell her to go pick up all my drops and do whatever she wants to do tonight because I'm in for the night at my mother's. I tell her I can't talk right now, and that a lot of shit has happened. She calls my mama's house. I answer just so she won't think I'm lying, and I tell her I'll call her when shit calms down. I tell her not to worry, just to go and pick up my money. She finally hangs up.

Nikki puts her arm around me and ask me is she can do anything. I shake my head, then I change my mind and tell her to go to the car and get the drinks and junk food. She does.

My mom and dad finally come out of the house and ask 101 questions. I just look at them and say, "Everything is okay now; please just leave me alone."

They know me better than to keep questioning me, so they leave me alone.

My phone is still ringing. Pops is blowing me up. I just turn it off, I need to clear my head.

I get in the Eldorado and put the top down. I turn on the DVD and a porno comes on while 2pac is jamming just for me, at least, that's what it feels like. I hit 96 while my mind travels at 1,000 mph and tears run down my face. I feel so lonely even though it seems like I have everything. Something is missing and I want to figure out what it is.

About 30 minutes later I pull up in front of Landy's house, park, fix my face and call her house. She comes out the door as the phone rings, gets in the car, looks at me and says, "What the hell has happened now?" I just shake my head and start talking while I hit Southfield freeway to Plymouth and pull up in front of the liquor store. Landy is laughing at me.

"What's so funny, bitch?"

"You, with your crazy ass. You really like the dude, huh?"

"No, I don't." I say.

"You're lying, bitch." She tells me like it is.

"Yeah, I think I am lying".

We get out the car and go into the store. We see the Arab who's been looking me up. He hallas for a minute, while some broke looking cats try to halla. We ignore them. I tell Al (the Arab) I'll see him next time.

We go back to the car and get in. I put Trina on and bump it as loud as I can without blowing the speakers. Landy is making the drinks. Two minutes later we're at the Park. It takes about 20 minutes to find a parking space. We park up, get out the caddy, sit on the hood and start getting wasted.

"Damn, you see that nigga over there, Crystall?" She and my family are the only ones who call me by my first name; not in front of people though.

"Where?" I ask, looking round.

"Over there with the Black Jag and all those niggas shooting dice; he's the one with the wife beater on!" I look over and guess who I see? Yes, motherfucking Pops himself!

"Let's roll out, it's time to go!"

"Why? What the hell's wrong with you now?"

"That's the ol' boy, Pops, the one I told you about!"

"Oh shit, fuck him girl, he doesn't even see you. Does he know this car?"

"Not sure," I say, "but if you look around, there ain't too many white bitches in here in a drop-top green El-dog on gold-ds is there? I'm kind of hard to miss, don't you think?"

"Shut up, bitch! So, what do you want...to go to the Isle?"

"Good idea." I say.

I get in and start the car. I put in *Hot Girl* by Juvenile and then, when I'm about to pull out, I see his ass standing right in front of my car.

"Oh shit," Landy says.

"Pops, you'd better move or I will run your ass over, you know that, don't you?" I yell out.

He stands there like I'm joking, then comes up to the driver's side, reaches in and takes the key out of the ignition.

"You ain't leaving until you talk to me. Not this time."

"Vanilla, I'm going to go halla at Fresh over there while you talk. Call me when you're ready, dog. And Pops, please don't piss her off, the bitch can't drive as it is!" Landy says.

"Shut up, Landy. You're just going to leave me like that, dog?"

"It's your love triangle, not mine. You've got to work this shit out on your own. Peace!" She makes me a drink, makes herself one, and then goes over to talk to one of our homies who's here in the park.

I tell Pops to get in so he won't make a scene. He laughs, gets in, reaches over and kisses my forehead. I jump back and say, "Please don't do that." I look around the park to see if anybody is paying us any attention.

"Who are you looking for, one of your girlfriends?"

"No, I just don't want these nosey folks in my business." I say, while I snatch the keys and turn on the ignition. I roll the top up and turn the radio on.

"What is there to talk about, Pops?"

"That's not one of your girlfriends too, is it?" He asks about Landy.

"No, that's my rawdog, she not gay either." I smile while I say that. "So what do you want?"

My phone rings.

"Excuse me." I say.

"*Vanilla's Ladies*." I say. "Hey Larry, yes Destiny is working. She's at 96 and Middlebelt with another girl if you know what I mean?" I fake a laugh while I talk to one of the clients. It's been a slow day, as it usually is on a Sunday.

"You want both of them? The whole nine yards, huh? You've got it baby. I'll call them and tell them you'll be there in 30 minutes. Alright Larry, have fun! Yes, the negotiation fee hon, $1,200 for both. Ha-ha-ha." I really fake laugh and finally hang up.

"I need to change professions. Shit, these motherfuckers really pay G's for some pussy, huh?" Pops says, trying to be funny.

"Yeah?!" I answer like he's stupid. "I've got to call my girls, hold on." I dial the number.

"Destiny? You and Suhey have got Larry coming in 30 minutes. $1,200 split three ways, alright?"

"Cool" she says. Then she asks me if I've heard from Spin. Destiny has been calling her phone all day and she hasn't been answering.

"No, the last time I saw the crazy bitch was when I threw her out of my house earlier today."

"That's why she's not answering her phone then, huh?" she says.

"I guess so. She'd better not come to me asking for money either. If her ass doesn't want to work, fuck it, I don't give a shit."

"You've got problems. I don't want anything to do with it. You'll be alright in a few days, if not hours."

"Alright girl, I'm in the middle of something, I'll call you back later if I get another client for you. If not, see you tomorrow."

"Alright, goodnight Vanilla." She says.

"Goodnight, you."

I finally hang up and look at Pops, he's still laughing.

"What's so funny?" I ask him.

"What you do for a living is funny to me, it just seems too easy, and too good to be true. What's the catch?"

"You've got jokes, huh? You say how easy it is, but you still want me to give it all up for you? I say and start laughing, lighting a cigarette and sipping my drink. "By the way, it's not as easy as you think it is, you don't know the whole story behind what I have to put up with; these crazy-ass women. I'm losing my mind here in these last few days, and you ain't helping either. Why do you want me anyway?" I just look at him and wait for an answer.

"What I want I obviously can't have." He says while he sips my drink. "I told you what I want, I told you how I feel, but you do nothing but push a nigga away. We can make shit happen together baby, you know that!"

He slides his hand between my thighs and just being near him makes me hot. I'm about to move his hand but I don't.

"Damn you're hot down there." He says, while he laughs.

I move his hand this time.

"You got into it with one of your girlfriends, huh?"

"Are you trying to be a smart ass?" I ask him seriously.

"No, just making conversation baby." He sips my drink again. I pop the trunk button and tell him to go and get a cup out of the trunk.

"You ain't going to pull off on a nigga, are you?"

"I ain't going to leave my girl here, am I?"

"Hell, you might." He says, but he gets out and goes and gets the cup. He tries to get back in the car. I lock the doors, laughing at him while he's looking serious as hell until I finally let him in.

"At least you do have a sense of humor. You're just going to lock me out like that?" He says, while he leans over and kisses my lips softly, I kiss him back.

"Pops baby, I ain't going to front, I want you. I want you bad. But this ain't going to work. It can't possibly work. It's bad enough I'm in two relationships already, but one is shaky as hell right now, because the bitch is crazy and already jealous as hell over you. That's what our fight was about this morning. I told her about what happened with ol' boy."

"Who, Nikki?" he asks.

"No, no, no, Spin, crazy ass, the one you met at the club. She was accusing me of fucking you and shit. And she's right. She doesn't even know about Nikki. Nikki knows about her and still wants to be around me for some reason. But I know I'll lose her too if I mess with you, and that means losing money. These are not just my women, they're my money. My top girls. I can't replace them that easily."

"From what I saw at the club, you've got no problem getting girls. I saw you and Simone exchange numbers."

"You know her?" I ask, suspicious.

"Just from the club, and she doesn't fuck with anybody like that. She comes in makes her money and bounces. You must have made an impression on her."

"She's been working for the last two days." I tell him, while hitting a Newport, and making another drink for me and him.

"Straight up?" I ask.

Pops nods.

"She called me the next day, asking when she can start. She got straight to business. I like her, and she's making a bank."

"You're telling me you'd rather be with two women because they're your main money-makers than to be with a real man, even though you're falling in love with him?" He says all sure of himself.

"Don't get a big head. And who said I was falling in love with your old ass?"

"I've been around long enough to see when a woman is in love with my old ass." He kisses me again, driving me crazy.

I kiss him back then jump like crazy and look at the window. It's Landy, with Fresh and a whole bunch of niggas we grew up with. She's drunk as hell.

"Bitch, you scared me! What the hell do you want?"

"Damn, first you don't want me to leave, now you kicking me out and shit? Are you letting him run game on you, dog?"

"Yeah right, you can't run game on the Queen of the game" I tell her while I look over at Pops. He laughs.

I get out the car, put the top down, hug my boy Fresh and say, "what's up?" to everybody. Pops gets out the car, passes me my drink.

"Thank you, baby" I say, and then I introduce Pops to my peoples.

"Damn V, your ass is getting fatter every time I see you, dog! What you been doing?"

"Fuck you, Fresh."

"I've been trying for years, but you like what I like so I gave up! Where's Spin's crazy ass at anyway?"

"Probably in hell; I don't know and I don't want to know. I hope she stays where she's at tonight!"

"You got into it again?"

"I don't want to talk about the bitch right now."

"You'll be alright tomorrow!"

"I doubt it. As soon as she finds out about this…"

"About what?"

I walk over to Pops and put my back towards his front and grab his hand with my free hand and lean my head back, looking at him, while I say, "him". Then I kiss him. He looks shocked but smiles.

"Damn, dog, I don't know what you did but whatever you did, you did right and I'm glad you did it!" He gives him some play.

I roll my eyes at both of them, get in the car and put Trina in - *Niggas ain't shit*. I laugh while they kick it. Landy jumps in.

"Are you going to fuck with him for real? What about Spin, and the new girl, whatever her name is?" She asks.

"Her name is Nikki, and fuck Spin. Yes, I'm going to fuck with him. If they leave I've still got six girls working, so fuck it, as long as he doesn't want me to give my shit up, we're going to be alright. I'm really falling for him, ain't I?"

"Yes, you are, bitch. I'm glad you've come back to dick for good!"

"Fuck you Landy!"

"No thank you, you ain't the right gender!"

"Funny, bitch."

I make us another drink and get out the car. About two cars down, some dude has got his trunk open, thinking of bumping his sounds. I look over at Landy and say, "Should I do it, dog?"

"Do it, dog!"

"It may hurt his feelings!"

"That's the point, do it!"

Pops is listening to us, looking confused. I open my trunk and bump Trina so hard the nigga next to us jumps. My shit killed his shit in two seconds. He looks over, mad, gets in his ride and closes the door. Everybody laughs.

"You're wrong" Pops tells me.

"Don't hate the player, hate the game." I jump up and kiss his cheek. He smiles.

"Alright dog. We're about to bounce, I've got money to make." Fresh tells me.

We all say bye and about two minutes later it's just me, Landy and Pops.

"Did you drive here?" I ask him.

"Yeah, but my brother's with me, why?"

"Which one is your brother?" Landy's drunk ass asks.

"The one with the wife beater on; he looks just like me. Why?"

"I'll be back!" Says Landy.

We laugh and lean against the car. I turn the music down and tell him I've got to use the phone. I call Sophia and tell her I'm going to be late. I ask Pops if he is leaving with me?"

"What about your girl?" He replies.

"Can she leave with your brother or something?" I holla at him.

"Hold on a minute. As a matter a fact come with me, you need to meet him anyway.

"No, I'll wait here", I say, and try to get in the car, but he stops me.

"Oh no, I want you to meet my people too. I met yours, didn't I?"

"Alright."

"Put a smile on your face girl, you look mean as hell."

"Good, maybe they won't talk to me."

He just laughs. I roll the top up, close the trunk, lock the doors, grab my purse and my phone, and walk with him. I've got everybody staring at me hard as hell. Pops loves every minute of it. We get over to his car and I can see Landy trying to run game on Pops' little brother.

"Kevin, this is Vanilla. Vanilla, this is my little bro, Kev; my cousin, Dre, and my nephew Dru."

"Nice to meet you." I give them all a fake ass smile.

"Damn girl, you're cold, ain't you?"

"What's that supposed to mean?"

"Leave my baby alone; that's why I like her, 'cause she's cold as ice. She's got plenty of heart."

"I heard about you girl," Kevin says.

"What have you heard?"

"You're a crazy white bitch!" Landy's drunk ass says.

"Suck my dick, bitch." It's a personal joke between the two of us.

"I will if you get one, hoe." They all laugh.

"You want another drink, baby?"

"She doesn't need any more." Landy says, trying to be funny.

"Your drunk ass doesn't need any more. And, by the way, do you mind if Kevin drops you off? You don't mind, do you Kev?" I smile really big.

"It's on you girl."

"Where are you going?" Landy asks.

"Pops is rolling with me."

"Uh, okay."

"Shut up," I tell her silly ass.

"Peace out, dog." She raises her cup to me and takes a sip.

"Alright dog, call me if you need me."

Pops gets his shit together and we walk over to my car. I pop the lock and get in. I roll the top down, pump Trina and roll out, not knowing yet where we're going. About five minutes later I turn the music down and ask him where he wants to go.

"Wherever you want to go," he says.

"Let's go to your place, Terrell Hardgrove." I say his full name and smile.

"Let's go then Crystal Vanilla Brownstone." He answers me, saying my full name. I just laugh.

"So where do you live?" I ask him.

"Troy," he says.

"You're close to me." I reply.

"Yeah, I know that."

"Do you, Pops? That was my mother's house you came to the other night."

"I know that as well, Crystal. You live in Novi."

"What don't you know?" I ask him, with a cheeky smile on my face.

"What you're going to do about Spin and Nikki is what I don't know," he says and looks at me seriously.

"I'll handle that, don't worry about it."

I think about what the hell Spin is doing and how she's going to handle this. I'm not really worried about Nikki, we just started this, and she'll get over it, if she even cares. I hope Spin hasn't done anything stupid after what happened today.

Chapter 7:

Pops tells me what exit to get off and where to turn, then finally, about thirty minutes after leaving the park, we pull up in front of a mini mansion.

"Well, I'll be damned." I say. "You're living good! How many bedrooms have you got?"

"Enough for you, me and the 5 or 6 kids we're going to have." He says, then kisses me and gets out.

"You've really lost it now."

"Nine rooms, five bathrooms," he finally answers.

"Shit, I'm moving in."

"Whenever you're ready."

"How old are you Pops?"

"Does it matter?"

"No, but I would like to know."

"Thirty-six. Is that too old for you?"

"You just made it, by one year," I tell him and laugh.

"Oh yeah, what is it, the 'thirty-five and over only' club?"

"Something like that."

"Spin and Nikki don't look thirty-five and over."

"They're not men, are they?" I say, trying to be a smart-ass.

My phone rings.

"Excuse me," I tell him and walk away to one of the other rooms.

"Hey Nikki, what's up baby?" I don't think I can do this. Hearing her voice breaks my heart.

"Vanilla, we need to talk." She sounds serious as hell.

"About what? Talk to me, baby."

"Not on the phone, in person. Where are you at?"

"I'm with Pops." I can't lie any more.

"I figured that. Spin told me what happened today between you."

"How and when did you talk to her?" I'm loud as hell now and I come back out to the room. Pops is in another room making a drink. He looks at me and smiles, but it changes to a frown when he sees my face.

"Well, I got her number off your cell phone the other night when we were together. I decided to call her. We met each other and decided we were going to put this shit to an end. I thought I could do this but I can't, Vanilla. Spin won't either. She's right here. Hold on."

"You're a lying-ass white bitch! All you ever did was lie to me. Why? Over a nigga? A piece of dick? You were fucking her too. How long were you going to keep her away from me, huh? I wondered why I never got to meet the new girl even though I had met the rest of them. I bet you're fucking Suhey too, huh? What about Destiny? Those fake bitches smile in my face one minute and fuck you the next."

Spin is going off and I'm going to let her. She has the right to.

"Spin, you're right about most of it. I ain't going to lie to you any more baby. You deserve the truth. I want you to leave me so I don't have to do it and yes, I want to be with Pops. It's only been a few days since he and Nikki came into my life, but they've flipped it upside down and I knew that, sooner or later, it was going to be over between us. I love you enough to tell you the truth. Please don't hate me for what I did to you. Move on with your life, Nikki too. I don't deserve you. You're too good for me. I want both of you to find somebody who is going to appreciate your love."

"Don't worry, I already did thanks to you," Spin says, laughing.

"Oh yeah, who?" I ask.

"Nikki," she says seriously, and hangs up. I stand there looking at the phone, shocked as hell, for about a minute until Pops breaks the silence.

"Are you alright?" I jump when I hear his voice.

"Yeah, I will be."

"So, it didn't go too well, did it?" He asks me.

"Actually, they made it a lot easier for me," I tell him.

"How's that?"

"They're together."

I tell him the whole story. He looks kind of happy about it.

"I've got to call Sophia," I tell him.

I grab my drink and sit down. I kick my shoes back while he massages my feet.

"Sophia, baby, just do as I say, okay? I'll explain later. Don't book Spin or Nikki ever again. Don't answer the phone if they call you, okay?"

"Alright. You okay?"

"Yeah, I'm fine. I'll see you tomorrow. How many calls have you had?"

"I had two. Suhey and Destiny had one, and Ayanna and Simone had one together, I guess they're fucking now. Diamond had two."

"Well, I'll be damned! What's my drop for today?"

"Two thousand, eight hundred," she says.

"Cool. Keep five hundred for yourself. You're going to handle the phones from now on. I'll take care of you, alright?"

"You got it baby."

"See you tomorrow."

"Goodnight, V."

I hang up the phone and swallow my drink. I make another, then pick up the phone again and dial Spin's number. I tried to act like it didn't bother me, but I can't do it anymore. She will get a piece of my mind.

"You think you did some shit, huh, Spin?"

"What do you mean?" She answers, surprised.

"Bitch, you wouldn't be shit without me, just remember that. You can't do shit on this scene without going through me. All you've got left is a nine to five, if you can find one, or Michigan Avenue and Woodward, Bitch. Don't think you can even dance at the bars again as long as I'm in business, 'cause that's not going to happened either, for you or Nikki. You hoes are finished. You'd better move if you're even thinking about trying to make a dime in this business 'cause the 'D' belongs to me, hoe. Don't you ever, ever in your life, try to embarrass me or check me again, you got that?"

"Why do you have to go all out the way, Vanilla? Why can't I just do my thing?"

"Because I will always own you, Spin, and whatever comes with you, so if you want to work, you only work for me, bitch. Think about that, okay? Call me when you're broke. When you need to pay your rent or your school tuition or when you want to go shopping again. Nikki ain't going to do that for your ass, is she?" I slam down the receiver.

"Why would you do that to the girl? She's already hurt as it is." Pops says.

"You're on her side now? It's all your fault, if you ask me. If I never met you, this shit wouldn't be happening. As a matter a fact, all I have to do is pick up the phone and call her and, believe me, she will take me back 'cause she knows that, without me, she ain't shit in this city."

"That's not what I mean, baby. Just leave her alone, for our sake, let her be. Okay? I don't want to worry about you or any bitch ever again, or do I have to?" He sounds pissed now.

"Who are you yelling at?"

"I ain't about to argue with your crazy ass, but if you think you're going run back and forth from here to Spin, then you've got it all fucked up! I ain't one for these games, I'm too old for this shit. You'd better get your mind right, Ma!"

No he didn't! He just walked out on me!

"Pops, where the hell do you think you're going? I want to know what in your right mind made you talk to me like that."

"What? You expect me to sit here and listen to you talk to your women in my house and not say shit? You've got the game all fucked up, baby girl! You'd better make up your mind tonight, me or her. I ain't about to compete with no woman. Remember that." He tells me while he turns on the radio and the jazz flows in the background.

He takes his shorts off and jumps in the pool, water splashing me. I just shake my head. I still can't believe I let a man talk to me like that and, in a way, I like the fact that he speaks up for himself. That makes me wonder if, maybe, that's why I never pay the men in my life any attention; because they do what I say, and it's kind of exciting to see a man act like a man and not let me run over him. I can honestly say I love this man!

"Are you going to get in or what?" Pops asks me.

I lose my train of thought.

"No, I don't have a swimsuit with me."

"So? Nobody can see you in here, just go and grab one of my tees, or jump in with your thong on!" He laughs and splashes me.

"Oh, you want to play, huh?" I say while I take my clothes off and jump in with just my thong on, no bra. (I wasn't wearing one.)

He catches me and kisses me hard, driving me crazy. He lets me go and dives under the water. I feel him taking my thong off. I scream, but help him. I take off his wife beater and throw it in the water. He sits me on the steps of the pool and starts kissing my thighs and between my legs, driving me wild. He stays down so I beg him to make love to me and he does until I scream. The best part of it is that he cums with me. Now, you know that's the best sex you can have, when a man climaxes with you.

"Damn Pops, what are you trying to do to me?"

"Make you love me, that's all." He says and kisses me.

"Go and get me a t-shirt, baby," I tell him.

"Hold on a minute, let me go and get some towels."

"Alright."

I look around the back yard. It's huge and beautiful and the wood fence is about twelve feet tall, so there's no way anybody can see us. I can see myself living here, for sure!

"Here you go baby." He gives me a towel. "So what do you want to do tonight?"

"Let's go out of town, get away from all this shit for a minute."

"Well, shit, I've got to hit Arizona tomorrow night, but we can leave tonight instead."

"What are you going to AZ for?"

"Business," he says.

That's all I'm going to get, I guess. I think to myself.

"Let me call Sophia and see if she can handle shit for a few days while I'm gone."

"Do what you've got to do baby." He tells me.

I go into the house and call her.

"Sophia? Hey baby. Look, I've got to skip town for a couple of weeks. I'm leaving tonight. Can you take care of business for me? I trust you, but just so you know, every call will be recorded while I'm gone. It's not you, baby, I did the same shit with Spin, alright? That's my money; I have to protect it somehow. I'll take care of you when I get back. Call me if you need me, alright? Bye." I hang up, not really waiting for a reply.

"Okay, let's go to my crib so I can pack. I'll call my family on my way there, then we can bounce. Cool?"

"Yeah. I've just got one stop to make in the city. If that's alright with you? Come on, let's do this."

Chapter 8:

About 45 minutes after we leave Pops' place, we're on Seven Mile and Greenfield meeting somebody at the gas station. Pops gets out and says he'll be right back. I look at him and say, "Do I have to pull my gun out?"

"No baby, these are *my* people, we're cool." He leans over and kisses me.

About ten minutes later I get out the car. I walk up to the truck, my hand touching the gun in my purse, and say, "Pops, what's up baby?"

"Everything's cool, V, chill out. These are my people, I told you. You can get your hand off the gun." He laughs at me.

"Well, excuse me!" I say and walk away with an attitude and get in the car, slamming the door. I turn up the music. About two minutes later he gets in, smiling. The guy from the truck gets in too.

"Baby, chill out, okay? This is my cuz Kev. Kev, this is Vanilla, you met at the park, remember?"

I look at him and recognize the face from the park.

"What's up? I didn't mean to snap, it just seems like every time you get out my car and into somebody else's, I've got to pull my gun out and shit. I don't want to go through this shit anymore." They laugh.

"It only happened one time."

"Shit, that's one time too many, and every time I see you get in somebody's car, I'm going to think it will happen again."

"That's why I love you, crazy ass." He kisses my hand.

"Whatever Pops."

"See how she treats a nigga, Kev? I only told one woman in my life, other than her, 'I love you,' and all she's got for a nigga is, 'Whatever'."

"That's why you love her ain't it? She ain't going to kiss your ass, or jump when you say jump. You like the 'rude girl' attitude she's got!"

"Hell yeah, I do. This is going to be my wifey!"

"You're really tripping. Are we rolling out or what?" I say.

"Damn baby, chill out. We're about to leave. I just wanted to run something by you while my cuz is in the car, so you know the drill."

"What's up?"

"We're going to pick some shit up on our way back. Is that cool with you?"

"You think I didn't know that before we left the house? I know more about you than you think."

"I love you, Crystal."

"Yeah, I know," I say and lean over, kiss him, and say for the first time to a man other than my father, "I love you too."

He backs up, looking happy and surprised.

"You can cut out the 'love you' shit while I'm in here." Kev says. We laugh and stop kissing

"Let's roll out, baby."

"You be careful," Kevin says and gets out.

"Can you be quiet for one minute while I call my family, baby?"

"Sure, go ahead," Pops says and turns the radio off while I call my sister and my parents to tell them I'm going out of town for about two weeks. I tell them I will call them soon as I get to Arizona. I tell them I love them and hang up.

I turn the radio on, put on the jazz station, relax, and tell Pops to hit the highway. He smiles and hits the 7-mile to Southfield on our way to Novi, to my house, to pack my shit. I'm lost in deep thought and I'm so in love with this man, it should be against the law.

I ask God to guide me through all of this, and keep me, us, safe. Your wondering why I am asking God to keep me safe while I'm committing a crime? Well, for some reason, I believe he is watching over me, always has and always will be.

Pops pulls up right in my driveway. I look over at him and laugh. He smiles back, then leans over and kisses my forehead. We get out of the car and go into the house.

"Make yourself at home." I say to him.

"How do you keep this place so clean when you're always on the go?" He asks me, while he sits on my $6,000 couch.

I don't even sit that couch! But I don't say anything.

"Housekeeper," I tell him and go upstairs to my room.

"Make sure you pack some bikinis!" He screams behind me.

"Why don't you come up here and pick them for me?" I scream back.

He flies upstairs and I point to my swimsuit drawer. He picks about seven bikinis, the smallest ones.

"You don't have a thong swimsuit?"

"Where am I going to wear that in Michigan?"

"Right, right. Well we're going to buy some in Arizona."

"So everybody can see my ass?"

"They can see it, but they can't have it."

He comes over to me and grabs my ass.

"Alright, let me pack. Get me my suitcases out the closet by the stairs."

"Baby, we're only going to be going to for two weeks, you don't need your whole closet."

"Give me both of the suitcases, Pops, I can't wear the same shit every day. And grab my carry-on too."

"No, you ain't taking all this shit with you, baby, we're going to go shopping too. You ain't going to have room for all this shit."

"Yes I will. I'll just take an extra suitcase for the clothes we're going to buy."

"I'm going to go and have a drink. Please hurry up, it's already dark outside."

"No it ain't."

"Shit, it will be when you finish packing four suitcases!" He says, throwing my carry-on on the bed.

"Don't throw my shit like that! I paid $700 for that Tumi suitcase."

"Jesus Christ, baby, just pack your shit, please!"

"Shut up and go make me a drink."

He goes downstairs while I pack up. He brings my drink up and lies down on my bed watching me, while I'm running around like a headless chicken. I'm packing and talking on the phone to Landy, and calling everybody else I need to call. Finally I hang up and jump on top of him, kissing him and ripping his clothes off and making sweet love to my man. When I'm done, I look at him, kiss him and say, "A little something for the road." He laughs and kisses me back and tells me he loves me and that we need to get rolling.

"Take these to the car. We're taking the Impala; it's low-key."

"I was going to tell you the same thing, baby. Damn, you even think like me."

"Great minds think alike."

"Meet you in the car." I throw him the keys.

"Hurry up please!" He asks, begging.

"I am rushing babe, damn, give me a minute please!"

About fifteen minutes later, I finally get my ass out of the house and I knock on my neighbor's door. After a minute he comes out and I ask him to keep an eye on the house while I'm gone. He's a young guy who lives with his three-year-old daughter. He's always had a crush on me, but he knows I am, well, I *was* a lesbian, so he never tried too hard to get with me. He's cute Italian guy, twenty-six, named Terry. I give him a hug and tell him I'm going out of town for a couple of weeks. I tell him to check his mail box as I walk away. Pops is looking hard, I just laugh at him and he pulls off. I look back and see Terry pull an envelope out of his mail box, he smiles and waves at me while he puts the five $100 bills in his back pocket.

"You left the nigga some money?"

"Yes, my money, for watching my house, is there a problem?"

"Have you fucked him before?"

"Oh hell no, you can take me back to the crib if you're going to be talking that crazy shit, sounding just like Spin's crazy ass."

"Don't compare me to no bitch you were with. I want you to answer me about that ol' boy or I'll go ask him myself!" He yells, loud as hell, looking pissed off and doing a U-turn at the end of my block.

"Pops, what the fuck is your problem? No, I didn't fuck him; he thinks I'm a straight up lesbian, and that's the way I like to keep it. Plus he just got a divorce about three months ago. We're just fucking neighbors, damn!"

He sits there looking stupid, like he should.

"I'm sorry baby, the way he looked at you just made me mad. It took everything in me not to get out the car and whoop his ass." He finally turns back around.

"You're scaring me, you know that, right?"

"I'm sorry Crystal, I'm just jealous as hell."

"You need to quit this shit or this ain't going to work." I say, looking at him serious as hell, and turning the radio on. I turn it up so I won't have to listen to him anymore!

He turns the radio down and tries to talk to me.

"Baby, for real, I'm sorry I snapped."

"Are you going snap every time somebody looks at me or talks to me? I deal with a lot of people, Pops, and the funny part is going to be trying to convince them that I'm with a man now, which half of them won't believe until they see you. The other half is going to be mad at me, because of Spin. Believe it or not, she's everybody's favorite. She's America's sweetheart, and I'm just the bitch!"

"You still love her, don't you?"

"Of course I do, it doesn't happen overnight, but that doesn't mean I'll go back to her. Just drive. I don't want to talk about it, okay? Please?"

"Okay, baby. I'm sorry, V. I love you, you know that, right?"

I nod my head.

"Yeah!"

Just relax, shut up and drive please! I turn the music up and relax while my mind travels a hundred miles an hour. What am I getting myself into? I think about my whole life in general and, in a way, I'm getting tired of it; ashamed of it. And I know I'm taking a big chance by going out of town with Pops to handle his business. Even though I'm sure I'm going to get taken care of as far as money goes, the time I'd be looking at if we get busted scares me. I had my boy, Deon, check Pops' record for me. He did seven years before for a dope case and I ain't trying to go there. I just pray that we make it there and back.

"Baby, you want something?" Pops asks me and I jump.

"Sorry babe, I was thinking too hard." He looks at me and asks me again if I want anything from the store. I look at the clock, it's 10.47pm.

"Get me some Newports and some Henny, ice and Coke. And some Winter Fresh gum and a Henny blunt wrap."

"A blunt wrap? For what? I thought you didn't smoke weed?"

"No, not really, but I will tonight. Do you know somebody around here that's got some gans?" I ask him.

"Yeah, on the Mile," he explains. "My people from Plymouth have got some at the gas station; we'll go up to Plymouth and Meyers really quick when you come out the store. You ain't going to be tripping and shit are you?"

"Go get the stuff!" I say while I call Sophia and ask her how shit is going.

"Listen, baby, I may need you to send me some money once I get there, okay? Western Union."

"Alright, until then I'll just put it in the bank because I don't want to be responsible for all this money."

"Alright baby girl. I'll call you tomorrow. Keep up the good work. Have you heard from Spin?" I just had to ask.

"No, I haven't." She says, sounding scared.

"You'd better tell me if you do, you hear me?"

"I will."

"I ain't bullshitting, Sophia!" I scream into the phone.

"I will, I will, Crystal. I mean Vanilla!"

"Alright, I'll call you tomorrow." I hang up, trying not to look pissed when Pops gets in the car.

"What's wrong?" He asks, as soon as he gets in.

"Nothing!" I look at him and frown my eyebrows. "Let's go get the weed," I tell him and turn up the music.

"Are you alright? Who was that on the phone?"

"Sophia!" I scream over the music. Then I finally turn it down while he pulls out of the parking lot.

"Everything is cool. I just had to check on some shit, is that alright with you? I've still got business going on here you know?!"

"Alright, smartass," he says and playfully hits my arm, while I act like everything is groovy and turn the music back up. Five minutes later we are at the gas station. I tell him to park in front of the door while I run in. I go in and get three $50.00 glass jars of gan, some lime green and pink looking shit that smells beautiful. I throw the weed on Pops' lap and tell him to roll it.

"What makes you think I can roll?" he responds. "Shit, you'd better do it because I can't roll that well!"

"Fine, I'll try to roll it, but if I mess up, don't go laughing at me, alright? And you're smoking with me."

"You know I will." He laughs.

About five minutes later we are on the freeway and I'm still trying to roll the first blunt. I look over at Pops and he's laughing at me.

Emilia Szleszynska

"What's so funny? Can you do better?"

"Yeah, I can," he says, laughing. "And I can do it while driving too."

"I would like to see that shit," I say and hand him the blunt with the weed already in it. About thirty seconds later the blunt is rolled, perfect and ready to smoke.

"I thought you said you couldn't roll?" I look at him and roll my eyes while I dry the blunt.

"I lied," he says as he leans over and kisses my cheek.

"What else have you lied about?"

"Nothing, baby, I promise."

"You better not have, punk." I hit him on the shoulder while I light the blunt and take a long-ass drag then start coughing like crazy.

"You alright, baby?" Pops asks me, laughing at me.

"Yeah, I'm alright, I hope!" I say while I'm still coughing.

"Drink some water."

"Yeah!" I grab the water and down half of the bottle. I pass him the blunt. He hits it and starts choking like crazy. This time I laugh at him.

"That's some good shit, ain't it?" I say.

"Hell yeah!" He responds.

"Shit, we're going to have to stop somewhere and get a room for the night, then hit the road in the morning, baby, because I ain't driving high and drunk."

"Good idea. I'll look for some signs and see if we can get a room nearby."

"Alright, baby." He says. He turns the music up and passes me the blunt. By the time I find a Hotel sign, we are high as hell and haven't even touched the liquor yet.

"There's a Red Roof Inn somewhere off this exit, baby."

"I see it."

"I'm high as hell," I say and start laughing.

"Are you still going to drink?"

"Hell, yeah," I tell him, popping open the bottle and make two drinks. I make a toast.

"To our future,"

"To our future, baby," He says and takes a sip.

"Roll the other blunt, Boo." I tell him and sip my drink.

"Let's wait until we get to the room, V."

"Whatever."

I lay the seat back and relax and close my eyes until we get to the room. Pops goes and gets the room, and about five minutes later we arrive at the door of room 306. We relax, smoke, and drink, and before we even get to the sex part, we have passed out.

Chapter 9:

I wake up to the phone ringing.

"Hello," I answer, with the biggest hangover.

"It's check out time in thirty minutes. Are you staying or checking out?"

"We're checking out." I hang up and wake Pops up.

"Let's get out of here, baby, we've got to hit the road."

We take a shower together and I give in to Pops, who's begging me for a quickie. About thirty-five minutes later we are on our way down to the car. We head to IHOP to get something to eat.

"Stop at the gas station, I've got to get something for this headache. It's killing me."

"Alright, baby, just hold tight."

"You don't have a hangover?" I ask him, surprised.

"Nope, I only had two drinks; your ass finished the bottle!"

"Got jokes, huh?" I say while massaging my temples.

"You want me to go and get it?" He asks me when we pull up at the gas station.

"Yes, please," I ask him.

He goes and gets the bottle of Motrin and hands the whole bottle to me.

"Damn, my head ain't hurting *that* bad!"

"It's for the road." He says, laughing.

"Let's go get some food so I can take these."

We pull up in front of the IHOP. It's about 1:00pm.

By 2:00pm we are back on the road, my headache is almost gone, thank God!

"I've got to call Sophia, baby, turn the music down, please!" I scream over the music while dialing her number.

"Hey Sophia, baby, what's going on?"

"Same shit, busy as hell trying to book clients and do clients at the same time." She says, laughing but being serious.

"You're the only one who can do it, Mami!" I try to give her some words of encouragement.

"I don't see how Spin did this shit all day." She says, then realizes she shouldn't have said it. "My bad, I didn't mean to bring her up, and she did call, by the way."

"What did she say?" I ask, like I really don't care. But really I'm dying to find out.

"Not much, she just asked me if you told me not to book her or Nikki. I told her that you had. Then she cussed me out, called me all kinds of fake, back-stabbing bitches and hung up. I didn't even bother to say anything back; she's just mad right now."

"Good, don't say shit to that hoe. Call me if you need anything. How many calls have you had since last night?"

"Just me or everybody?"

"Everybody."

"Seventeen, baby. You're getting paid!" She's laughing hard.

"*You're* getting paid!" I tell her.

"Where are you at now?

"Girl, we're still in Michigan, we ain't going to be in Arizona for another four or five days, if not longer, at the rate we going." I say, looking at Pops. He's laughing at me for being a smartass.

"You be careful. I'll call you if anything pops up."

"Alright," I finally hang up and light a cigar, smiling.

"What's up? What are you smiling at?" Pops asks me, laughing.

"Nothing, I'm just trying to figure out how much money I made between last night and today."

"You didn't do shit!" He says, being a smart ass.

"Shit, I did all the work I needed to do when I put this shit together. It's supposed to be easy now."

"So how much money have you made?"

"None yet," I stick my tongue out at him.

"Straight up?"

"Straight up, stop counting my money nigga!" I say, laughing. I turn the music back up, blasting Jay-Z.

For the next few days, we will drive, eat on the road, and sleep in different hotels until we get to wherever we're going in Arizona. Hopefully it will be a pleasant trip. The fact that Pops is with me makes the journey more pleasant.

Finally, days later, we arrive in Tempe, Arizona, a city I never heard of, but this is where Pops takes care of his business. I've been in touch with Sophia every day. Business is booming, I had her put all of my drops in the bank and told her not to worry about Western Union, I've got my ATM card if I need some money. And I doubt if Pops will let me pay for anything anyway, which I really don't mind.

By the time I get back to the "D", my bank account is going to be like Wooh! I love it! I haven't really spent any money in over a week, so that will put a few extra Gs in the bank. And it gives me enough for me to go on a shopping spree. My family is going crazy without me, but I told them they're going to have to do without me for the next two or three weeks.

We finally get settled in at the Ritz. I spend most of my time shopping, tanning and talking on the phone to my sisters, Landy and Sophia. I call other people I really don't like, now and then, just to make them a little jealous and let them know how wonderful life is when you can make money and have a wonderful vacation at the same time. They act like they're happy for me, but they really ain't. They love to hate on me and I love it when they do it. I'm the bitch that you love to hate! By now I think the whole city knows that I dropped Spin and hooked up with Pops, which made a lot of women and men jealous and really not happy. Like I said, I love it when they hate on me!

I hope it won't hurt us in any way, as far as business goes. Pops and I don't really spend too much time together in the first few days. He's running around taking care of business and the only time I see him is when he comes in for a shower, changes his clothes and we have a quickie. Then he bounces, but not until he leaves me some money first. He refuses to let me pay for anything because he says this trip is on him. I'm not going to argue with him either.

Sophia is banking back in the "D". My new girls, Simone and Ayanna, are my new number one stars, as I call them. They're making me double the cut I usually get. My family is cool. I had Sophia drop off $5,000 at my mother's house since I've got some extra, extra cash this week.

Right now I'm at some little strip mall looking for something Pops might like. My baby likes simple things like wife beaters and shit, so I really don't know what to get him. I decide on some glasses, there's no place like D.O.C. I go in and pick out a matching pair of Guccis for both of us. It costs me (well, him) almost $1,800, but it was worth it. I get back to the room and Pops comes in about two hours later. I've already showered and changed clothes. I've got my hair and make-up done to go out and see AZ.

"Hey, baby!" I say to him while he walks in the door looking tired as hell.

"Damn girl, you look good!" He looks me up and down, licking his lips.

"I know, thank you!" I smile and kiss his cheek.

"Where are you going?" He asks, surprised.

"Wherever you take me!" I pout as I say it.

"You're right. You look so good tonight with that new outfit on; I've got to show you off to my peoples."

"You like?" I tease him while I model my new Gucci outfit for him, with my matching Gucci shades and purse.

"Damn Boo, how much money did you spend today?" He asks, laughing.

"Why? I'll pay you back if you want?"

"No, no, no, baby. Just asking!"

"About 9 Gs," I say really quietly.

"But I bought you something too!" I go and get the eyeglass case and give it to him. He smiles and opens it. "I got us matching glasses. Do you like them?"

"I love them, baby." He puts them on and looks in the mirror then tries to be a smartass as he says, "So you only spend a few hundred on your man and almost 10 Gs on yourself, huh?"

"Are you trying to be funny, huh?"

"No, just speaking the truth." He's really laughing now.

"Look, you're the only man, except my daddy, I even shop for. I don't know what you like, except for me of course!" I look at him seductively and I know he loves it.

"I guess we need to learn some things about each other then."

"I guess we do." I kiss him on his cheek, forehead and everywhere else I can on his face until we're on the bed making out. But then I remember my hair is done and I get back up.

"What's wrong?" He says, looking surprised.

"Oh, nothing, I just don't want to mess up my hair before we go out," I say, smiling while fixing my lipstick in the mirror.

"You're a tease." He gets up and heads for the shower.

"I know. Hurry up, you've got thirty minutes, it's already 10:15pm. I want to party for at least three hours!" I scream over the shower as I sit on the bed watching 'Cops'. About twenty minutes later we're out the door to some club called *Shake Yo' Tail Feather*, and that's exactly what I'm going to do.

About twenty minutes later, we pull up in front of the club and valet park the Impala. The valet guy gives Pops props for the car so I have to tell him like it is.

"It's mine." I smile and walk towards the door, Pops is behind me, laughing.

"You just had to do that, didn't you?"

"Yup, don't try to get the props for my shit," I say to him, laughing, while walking in the club.

"I thought what's yours was mine and what's mine was yours?"

"It is, Pops!" I say and pay our way to get in; thanking God they didn't card me!

"Let's get a booth baby!" I try to scream over the music.

"Alright, I'll go get the drinks!"

"No, wait. There's a waitress!" I scream again. "Excuse me, Miss, can we get a booth and place an order please?"

"Sure, follow me!" She screams back.

"The VIP booths are $25.00. Is that okay?

"Yeah, that's cool!" I give her a head to toe look.

"Here you go. What do you want to drink?"

"Give me a bottle of Cristal and two double shots of Henny one Ice, with two Cokes on the side please!" I'm still screaming.

"You're doing it right, huh?"

"Always," I smile at her fine ass and watch her walk away looking sexy as hell!

"Why are you looking at her like that?"

"Don't start this shit, Pops." I look away smiling, he's jealous as hell!

"*You* don't start the shit here."

"Whatever. Please don't ruin this night. Here are our drinks, let's get drunk and dance." I lean over and kiss him nice, long and hard.

"You should get a room for that!" Our waitress tells us, laughing.

"We've got one already. Want to come with us after you get off work?" I ask her, serious as hell.

"Vanilla?! What the hell do you think you're doing?" Pops looks at me like I'm crazy.

"Shut up, baby, I'm recruiting." I explain. He laughs.

"Here's my business card, Ma, call me when you're ready to make some real money!" I tell her and hand her the card.

"Are you a pimp?" She asks, looking at Pops.

"Hell no!" he says, fast as hell.

"No baby girl, this is my Escort Business, so I guess you could say I'm the Pimp, but I won't call myself that, I'm a business woman. This is my fiancé."

"Are you from the 'D'?" She looks at the business card.

"Yeah, why?"

"Oh, nothing, I've got family there!"

"Call me at the room tomorrow if you want to take a road trip to see your family, on me!"

"I might take you up on that!" She says, smiling, showing those perfect white teeth, looking like Lisa Ray from the Playa's Club. All I can do is laugh.

"What's so funny?" She asks me.

"You look like one of my girls; that's all!"

"She must be fine then!" She laughs and walks away.

"You're something else, you know that, right?" Pops tells me, looking at me all funny and shit.

"Yup, that's why you love me!" I pop open the Cristal and pour some in our glasses and make a toast.

"To us, baby."

"To us," he says and we down the first glass.

"So, do you think she'll call tomorrow?" He asks me.

"Yeah, they always do!" I say, smiling hard, watching Lisa Ray watching me.

Damn, I don't even know her name. I'll ask her when she brings the bill. About fifteen minutes later she comes back to the table.

"I've made up my mind. You seem like good people. I'll call you tomorrow before 12:00am and we can roll out."

"Well we're going to stay here for a few more days but you can hang out with us if you like?" I look over at Pops, he nods his head.

"Here's my number, call me and we can meet up at my house tomorrow."

"Does that sound good…Ebony?" I read her name off the piece of paper she gives me with her number on it.

"Well I'm about to get off and chill for a minute. You're not leaving, are you?"

"No, not until I dance!"

"Come on let's hit the dance floor then, girl. Do you mind?" She smiles at Pops.

"No, you go ahead. V, let me halla at you for a second."

"Say what you've got to say, baby." I laugh and lean over and kiss Pops.

"Don't even think about it Crystal." He whispers in my ear.

"About what?" I ask.

"The lesbian shit, that's what!" He sounds angry as hell and squeezes my arm really hard.

"Let go of me, Pops!" I scream. He lets go and smiles, looking funny as hell.

I look pissed off, because, well, I *am* pissed off, but I turn around and smile at Ebony. We hit the dance floor making him more jealous than ever. I come back after two songs to get a drink. Pops asks Ebony if she will excuse us for a minute. She does.

"What the hell did you think you were doing up there with the dyke?"

"I was a dyke when you met me, don't judge me now! All I did was dance with the girl, Pops!"

"Freak dance, bitch!" He flinches like he's going to hit me.

"No you didn't. Don't ever, ever in your life, call me a bitch or raise your hand to me like you're about to hit me."

"Shit, babe, I'm sorry."

"Fuck you, Pops, I'm gone." I walk away from him. I run out to the parking lot. The valet gives me my key. I see Pops run out and run behind me to the car, I get in fast enough and lock the doors. I flick him off and pull out of the parking space, almost hitting someone. Thank God there was nobody blocking the driveway.

It took everything in me not to cry, but I finally break down. I drive for about an hour. Pops tries to call me about forty times, but I will not answer the phone. He leaves several messages. When I call the hotel to check if Sophia has called, I find out Pops called and left messages there too.

Finally I see a Holiday Inn. I pull up and get a room. I relax, take a shower and call the Ritz and leave a message for Pops at the front desk:

"I'm fine, don't worry about me. I'll pay you back for everything, have a good life. And, by the way, it's *Miss* Bitch to you, Halla!"

Chapter 10:

It's 9:46am. I can't sleep. Shit is running through my mind. My phone has been going off all night. I finally had to put it on vibrate because I got tired of listening to the damn thing ringing. Nobody's calling but Pops' bitch-ass. He must have got my message from the front desk already. I call the room back and they tell me he already left this morning but didn't check out.

That should give me enough time to go up there and grab my shit and take it back to my new room. I brush my teeth, wash my face, skip the shower, and put my clothes on as fast as I can. I hit the gas station across the street and get a map of the city so I know how to get back to the room. I have no idea where I'm going but I'll get there somehow.

Pops keeps calling me like crazy! He must have rented a car because I doubt he's taking a cab everywhere around a strange city. I'm almost at the room so I call again to make sure he's not there. Thank God he's not! I'm so glad I kept all my stuff in my suitcases and shopping bags.

I park in front of the door, pop the trunk open, run into the room and, about seven minutes later, pull out of the parking lot. That was a close one. I had no idea he would be pulling up as I turned the corner. Thank God he didn't see me! I'm sure he's going to be tripping once he sees all my shit is gone! I had to laugh hard at that one. Oooh! It felt good!

I put Trina on while I'm on my way to the room to shower and change. Shit, Ebony from the bar is supposed to meet up with us today. I pull the piece of paper she wrote her number on out my purse and call her and leave a message. I tell her to meet me at the room or at least call me back. I tell her not to worry about what happened last night, my man's not with me, it's just going to be me and her. I hope he hasn't fucked up my money.

I get to the room. About twenty minutes later my cell phone rings while I'm in the tub.

"Hello?" I answer, trying to sound sexy.

"May I speak to Vanilla please?"

"May I ask who's calling?"

"This is Ebony from last night," she responds with a morning voice.

"Hey baby, this is her, sorry about last night, he was drunk, jealous, and tripping. I've got my own room, I left the info on your answer machine, I hope you got it because I'm in the tub now," I say, laughing.

"Do you want me to come over now?"

"Yeah, I'll be done by the time you get here."

"Is your man going to be tripping again?" She asks me.

"Look baby girl, he doesn't run shit, okay? And, so you feel safer, he doesn't know where I'm at. I haven't spoken to him since last night."

"I'll be there in about an hour."

"See you in a minute, baby girl."

I hang up, get out of the tub and finally call Pops.

"What do you want? You got my message, didn't you?" I tell him with the fakest 'I don't care' voice I've ever used.

"Yeah, I did, Crystal. I was drunk baby, I was tripping, please come back to the room so we can talk?"

"Let me think about it… Uh, no! You think you can embarrass me like that and just say, 'I'm sorry'? Hell no! I've got business to take care of anyway. You'd better take a plane back to the 'D' because you ain't riding with me." I laugh, hard as hell.

"I've got a rental car, V!" He says, sounding pissed off.

"I know, a 2009 DTS Pearl, right?"

"How do you know?" He asks, surprised.

"I see you and you can't see me!" I hang up and laugh! Stupid ass!

We can play this game if he wants I say to myself while getting ready and waiting on Ebony.

About thirty-five to forty-five minutes later, there's a knock on my door. I look through the peep hole. It's Ebony.

"Hey baby girl." I open the door, smiling and smoking a Gold and Mild.

"What's up, V? Are you ready to roll out? Let me show you around town."

"That sounds good. Hold on, let me make a few phone calls first." I walk back into the room.

I sit on the bed and call home to check in with my family. They are alright. I call Sophia, and check on shit with the service; everything is cool, money is coming in really well. Spin and Nikki haven't called. For some reason I was hoping they had. Well, Spin at least.

"Is everything cool?" Ebony asks me.

"Oh, yeah. Let's go and get something to eat. Is that cool with you?"

"Yeah, let's go. I know this really good local joint, it's a hole in the wall place but the food is really good."

Emilia Szleszynska

"Let's roll," I say.

I grab my purse, keys and phone and close the door, on our way to the restaurant.

After a nice lunch of some real soul food, we are on our way to wherever my little heart desires. Pops has been calling me like crazy, but I just let it go to the voicemail. I'll call him later. I hate to say this but I miss him. Maybe he *was* just drunk and talking stupid. I miss his punk ass. I'll let him suffer for a few days then let him make it up to me for a week or so. It should be fun. Until then, I'll let Ebony entertain me.

"So, where do you want to go now, V?" She asks me.

"Let's go get some liquor and then hit the mall." I tell her while I park in front of the store.

"Alright," she says, smiling and lighting a Newport. About fifteen minutes later, I get back in the car with a bag full of goodies. I throw it on the back seat and pull off.

"I like you," I say and let the music take over the silence. She leans over and kisses me on the cheek looking like a five year old on Christmas day. I just laugh while she tells me how to get to the mall.

Four hours, and a $3000 broker later, we come out of the mall, cracking up. We had fun, but how can you not when shopping? Ebony even bought me something with my own money! Ain't that something?!

"So you want to come to the 'D' with me and see your family?"

"Whenever you're ready to leave," she says, smiling.

"Are you down to get paid?"

"Hell yeah! Well, as long as I don't have to shake my ass!"

"No, you don't have to do that. But if you do, it's going to be for G's, not $10.00 a dance, I promise. We get paid, okay? I'll let my main girl, Sophia, school you in and show you around. She's been with me for a while."

"How many girls have you got working?"

"I had eight, but now it's six. I had to let two go; too much drama."

"I won't ask what happened," she says. She must have seen the look on my face when I said that.

"What's up with the ol' boy you were with?"

"Pops? That's my man. He does his thing, I do my thing, he makes his money, I make mine, and we don't get into each other's business. He's a little jealous though because I used to be with a woman before him. To be honest with you, he's the only man I've ever been in love with, or even in a relationship with." I laugh as I say that, thinking of Pops.

"I'm gay as hell too, I guess." She says. "I won't fuck with just anybody though. Those hoes are nasty to nasty these days… I like classy women, not trashy." She says while stroking my cheek with her hand.

"Baby, I don't get down any more, business is business, and me and Pops are about to get married. I ain't going to lie, you're tempting as hell and I do want you, but you and I both know we'd rather make money together than have sex, right?" I hope it will work.

"Right, but it would be nice if we could do both!" She laughs. "Just teasing you, V" She laughs hard. I laugh with her while we are on our way to her house.

"Here we are," she says, grabbing her bags and getting out. "Do you want to come in?"

"No thank you, I've got to meet Pops. He's going to kill me if I keep ignoring him," I laugh.

"Alright girl, call me when you're ready to bounce to the 'D', alright?"

"Alright baby girl."

She gets out the car and I finally call Pops.

"About fucking time you called me. How long were you going to ignore me, V?" He demands as soon as I get on the phone.

"Longer than this I thought," I say, laughing.

"So, have you seen the ol' girl from the bar?"

"Yup, I just dropped her off. She's coming to the 'D' with us too and no, I didn't fuck her. I told her it's strictly business. She's cool with that. I even told her we were getting married." I really laugh at that one.

"What's so funny about that?" He asks me.

"Nothing, it just sounds funny, me getting married to a man."

"Ha-ha, Vanilla." He fake-laughs.

"F. U. Pops."

"Shit, you need to. I miss you, Mami!"

"I miss you too. Meet me at my new room." I give him the direction.

About thirty minutes later, he knocks on the door. That's one knock I should never have answered because it started the biggest mess in my life. The beginning of Hell! I made a mistake taking Pops back and I will pay for it in the long run. I should have let the fool go at the night at the club. A few months later I find out what he's really about.

Chapter 11:

"You'd better tell that hoe to stop calling here, Vanilla!" Pops is yelling at me.

"She works for me. I can't tell her not to call, Pops! You're going to fuck up my money!" I'm pissed now, and yelling at him.

"Your money, huh? Fuck her and your money; you get rid of the bitch! Send her back to Arizona. All she wants is to fuck you anyway!"

"Whatever. We all know that ain't going to happen and she gave up before we even got back to the 'D'."

"I heard the bitch on the phone, Crystal; she thinks she can get one over on me!"

"I can't take this shit, Pops. You're crazy! You're tripping too much! That shit ain't cute anymore. Why are you so worried about her anyway? My other girls call here all day too!"

"They ain't trying to fuck you!" He snaps.

"How would you know?" I snap back!

"Are they, V?"

"They always have. I ain't changed shit since you came around, except that now Spin is gone!"

"So, are you fucking any of those dykes?"

"Hell no, you did *not* go there again! I'm out of here! I've got to go collect my money from 'those dykes'!"

"Bitch, don't walk away from me!" He grabs my neck and throws me against the wall. I lose my train of thought.

"You're going to get your ass whooped if you don't act right, V. Try me!" Then he storms out the door. I am so shaken up I don't know what to do. I watch him leave in his Jag.

About two minutes later, I leave to go and see Ebony and Sophia to pick up my drops. I try my hardest to act like nothing happened.

Pops doesn't come home that night. In the morning, when he does, he smells like another bitch too!

"Did you have fun last night?" I ask, smiling.

"Don't start that shit, V"

"She was kind of cute, you should have brought her home; I might have wanted to fuck her too."

"What the fuck are you talking about?" He looks confused, but shocked at the same time.

"The bitch you were with last night! It's cool because, trust me, I get more pussy than you ever will!" I yell and slam the door while he's standing on my front porch looking stupid.

Good - he really believes I saw him with a bitch and he didn't even deny it. The Bastard! Why can't I just leave his ass! What is wrong with me? Why am I going through this shit with his old ass? I break down crying.

I want to call Landy, but I'm too embarrassed to tell anybody about how I let this man treat me. For some reason, I'm scared to leave him because I don't know what he might do if I try. Really, I don't want to leave him, I want things to be the way they were when we first met (without the shooting part!). He was so different. I wonder if this is why he was single, because he flips the script once he knows he's got the female head over heels in love with him. And, to be honest, he's got me. I try to talk to him and scare him a little bit; make him think I'm gone if this shit happens again. It may work. (I doubt it.)

"V, please open the door!"

"Why should I? So you can hit me, Pops?"

"Baby, you know I won't hit you. Come on, Crystal!"

I finally open the door; my suitcases are next to the couch, right by the door.

"Where are you going?" He asks, looking shocked.

"Home," I say and go upstairs to finish packing. I run out of suitcases so I use garbage bags. He runs upstairs behind me.

"Come on, Crystal, it's not that serious, Ma."

"For you it's not, for me my life is serious, Pops. You don't have to worry about me putting my hands on you. I do, on the other hand. I'm not going to wait until you finally beat me half to death, okay?!" I say while I'm still packing. He just sits there looking stupid, not saying anything for a change.

"So it's over, huh?" He finally speaks.

"If that's what you want, Pops, I just thought that we needed some time apart, I was going to move back to my house full time and we can try to work things out, but if you want it to be over that's cool with me!" I look at him and smile, while I keep on packing.

He finally gets up, walks over to me, kneels by me and puts my hands on his face and just looks at me, makes my whole body melt. I love this man.

"Baby, I never want this to be over, *never*! Crystal. I love you and I'll be damned if I let you get away that easily. Do you really want to move out?"

"I think it's a good idea for now."

"Please wait until tomorrow night. I've got a surprise for you, please, before you take all your stuff."

"Okay, but only until tomorrow," I say and push the full bag into the closet. "Pops…?"

"Yeah baby?"

"Are you cheating on me? Please don't lie to me. Please tell me if you've been fucking somebody!"

"Hell no, how could I, with you on my ass twenty-four, seven? And why would I with a dime piece like you at home?" He walks over and hugs me, grabbing my ass.

"I just want you to know that I don't believe a word you say any more, you're going to have to make me trust you again. It's not going to be easy." I say my piece and go downstairs and watch a basketball game, ignoring Pops, acting like he ain't even there. He sits next to me and asks me if I want him to make me a drink.

"No, I'm tight," I say, never taking my eyes off the TV. "As a matter of fact, I'm about to go to sleep. I'll see you tomorrow; I'll be going to before 2:00pm, alright?" I smile at him and walk upstairs.

I feel him following me. I lie on the bed, turn the radio on and close my eyes while he stands there watching me from the doorway.

"Are you going to stand there watching me all night?" I finally ask.

"I could, you're so beautiful, Ma." He smiles then finally walks over and starts kissing my feet and massaging my whole body. I relax while my face is in the pillow laughing. The only reason I stayed is because I want some good loving and I can't think of anybody to call right now who will give me some as good as this. It seems like the whole world knows me and Pops are together now and I'm not going to take the chance just to fuck anybody so he can try to really kill me if he finds out. I could, of course, go and see one of my girls but I want this dick at least one more time.

I don't know why, but my woman's instinct is telling me Pops is fucking around and I will find out sooner or later. Until then we can both play the game. The fool thinks he can play me at my own game? We'll see who wins.

Chapter 12:

I wake up at 10:14am. Pops is still knocked out. I take a quick shower and when I get out he is up and on the phone. I don't say a word to him; I just get dressed and sing under my breath until he finally speaks.

"Baby, please meet me here at 8:00pm, okay? No, make that 9:30pm, just so I have enough time for everything since it's such a short notice of you moving out."

"I told you 2:00pm, Pops."

"Come on, V, please, just be here." He's begging now. I like this.

"Alright, I'll be here. I've got to go take care of some business. I'll call you when I'm on my way."

"Alright baby, I've got to get going." He says while he jumps in the shower.

"Well, I'll see you later, I'm gone!" I yell on my way down the stairs.

"Love you, V."

"Whatever, Pops," I yell and roll my eyes.

The fool thinks he's slick. I wonder what he's up to this time. What's he going to try to bribe me with? I guess I'll wait and see.

I've had a long-ass day, but a good day. I hope Pops doesn't mess it up. It's 7:30pm. I'm walking in the house, about to take a shower and change clothes. I wait on him to come home while I finish packing all my shit, because no matter what he does, I'm still moving.

Finally, at 8:46pm, I hear his Jaguar in the driveway. He looks really nice with his Gucci loafers on. He's wearing some cream slacks, a wife beater and the Gucci glasses I bought him. He walks in, smiling hard, with a box the size of a cake box in his hands. He puts it on the table and comes over to me and kisses me, telling me I look beautiful. We talk for a minute. I see him looking out the window so I ask him if he's waiting on somebody.

"Yes, I am," he says, smiling.

"Who are you waiting on?" I ask, aggravated.

I don't have time for this shit to unpack. It's going to take me two trips to take this shit over to my house anyway. Then, as soon as I say that, two cars pull up and one of them is Pops' brother with some female, the other is his cousin Kevin with his nephew Dru.

"What the hell are they doing here?" I ask looking confused and even scared for a minute.

What is this man up to?! I don't trust him far as I can throw him.

"What's up, V!" Kevin walks in and hugs me. Everyone else comes in after him, hugging me and being nice and shit. Dru's got a bottle of Black Ace Champagne in his hand, smiling hard. I finally look over at Pops. He walks over to the table and picks up the cake looking box and comes towards me asking me to sit down.

"Why?" I ask, looking confused.

"Just do it, V, please!"

"You're scaring me, Pops." They all start laughing.

"Baby, please do it!" He's laughing too now. "I'm nervous already," he says, his hands shaking.

"Okay." I finally sit down.

"Crystal, baby, we've had our ups and downs like every couple, but we always get through it and I hope we can get through this too. I've made some stupid mistakes and I'm sorry for them, baby, please give me a second chance. I love you so much girl." Then he gets down on one knee and opens the cake box and pulls a small ring box out. He opens it, and I seen a big-ass pink diamond looking at me saying, 'You'd better say yes!'

Then finally, with his voice shaking, he asks, "Crystal, will you marry me?"

I stay there, looking at him like I'm stupid or can't speak.

"Baby, did you hear me?!" Pops asks.

"Yeah, I heard you," I finally say, an eternity later.

"Girl, you'd better say yeah; look at that ring!" Kevin's girl says to me.

"Yes Pops, I love you too, Papi." I finally get the words out of my mouth and let him put the ring on while Dru pops the Black Ace.

"The glasses are in the cabinet in the dining room." I tell him.

They all clap while I still sit there looking stupid and don't have anything to say for the first time in my life.

"You okay, Mami?" Pops asks me.

"Yeah, give me a minute… and a drink," I say and grab a glass of champagne from Dru.

"Get me a real drink somebody, please." They laugh. Kevin walks over to the bar and makes me a double shot of Henny, just the way I like it.

"To the newly-weds!" Dru, stupid ass, tries to make a toast.

"They ain't married yet dumb ass!" Nadia, Kevin's girlfriend, says to Dru while we all crack up.

"To the newly-engaged!" Kevin says, and we all drink our glasses of champagne, then I down my Henny like I've never done before. I go and make myself another one.

"So, when is the wedding day?" Nadia asks.

"Not for a while," I say looking at Pops. He just laughs.

We all kick it for about fifteen minutes then everybody finally leaves except me and Pops. We've got a lot to talk about.

"So are you still moving out on me?" Pops finally asks me.

"I don't know, baby, I think we need a little time apart because you've been tripping lately."

"That's not going to happen again, V. I'm not going to hurt my wife." He comes by me, puts his hands on my ass and kisses me really hard, making my whole body melt. He's good at doing that.

"Well, I guess I can stick around and see if things get better. But if you keep on tripping like you have been and calling me out my name, Pops, and coming in at five or six in the morning smelling like some other hoe's cheap perfume, I'm gone!" I'm almost yelling by now.

"You don't have to yell at me, Ma, chill out!" He pouts and kisses me again.

Damn, I've got a weak spot for this man! I still don't trust his ass all the way, but I believe we can get through this as long as he keeps his shit tight.

"Damn, my hand hurts, baby!" I laugh, looking at my ring. "How much did you pay for this?" I ask him, seriously.

"Wouldn't you like to know?!" He smiles and makes both of us another drink.

"Come on, tell me!" I'm doing the pouting now. "I'm going to get it appraised anyway, punk!" I get up holding my hand up and get on the phone, calling Landy and Sophia. I'll tell my family in person.

"Who are you calling?" He asks.

"Sophia and Landy; is that okay with you?"

"Yeah, I guess so." He turns the volume up on the TV while I share my good news with my girls. Fifteen minutes later, I'm off the phone and sitting next to Pops on the couch.

"Baby, are you going to help me unpack?"

"Well actually you may want to leave some of it packed because we need to go back to Arizona next week anyway."

"Already?"

"It's money, honey" He smiles and dials a number on his cell phone.

"Well I guess I'll unpack some of this shit. I go upstairs and start hanging my clothes back up; the ones I'd stuffed in the garbage bags. About an hour later I'm done. Finally, I go back downstairs and Pops is still on the phone. About five minutes later, he grabs his car keys and tells me to come on; we've got a move to make.

"Right now? I'm starving!"

"We'll get some food on the way." He says smiling.

"Should I change?"

"No baby, come on, you look fine, and we're going to be late!"

"Late for what?" I ask.

"Just come on, V!"

"Where are we going at 10 past 10 at night?"

"You'll see," he says while we are on the freeway.

"Alright, this better be good!" I turn the radio up and relax while fixing my makeup and hair, since Pops was a little rough kissing me and shit. At 10:39pm we pull up in front of Club 2000 and valet park the Jaguar.

"Why are we here? I told you I was hungry as hell!"

"You're going to eat, I promise!" He grabs my hand and drags me in the door laughing.

"Shit, I'd better eat soon, I know that!" I'm really whining now.

"SURPRISE!" I hear about 200 people yelling.

I look around and see Sophia, Suhey, Diamond, Ayanna, Simone, Destiny, Fresh, Chill, Landy, and whole bunch of the people I grew up with as well as Pops' people.

"Congratulations Vanilla and Pops!" My boy D.J. Tax screams over the microphone.

"Why did you do this to me, Pops?!" I ask him looking mad as hell, surprised and happy at the same time.

"Because I love you!" He kisses my forehead and tells me to enjoy myself and he'll be right back. He's got to go and kick it with Kevin for a minute.

"Well, I'll be over there cussing out my people and trying to get some food!" I'm yelling over the music now.

"Alright, Ma!"

"Why didn't you tell me anything?" I ask Sophia and the girls.

"Shit, I didn't know until this morning when Pops called me and asked me to call everybody; so I did and here we are!" She throws her hands in the air pointing at everybody. "Girl, let me see that ring!" Sophia grabs my hand and smiles from ear to ear. "Damn the nigga loves you girl!"

"Shit, he'd better" I smile and laugh with all my people.

"Damn, does Pops know all these people, or is it an open door party?"

"It's open door girl; you didn't really invite all these people did you?"

"Shit, I hope not! I don't want all these motherfuckers at my wedding!" I laugh. "I'll be back; I've got to get some food!" I walk over to the bar after being stopped by like 50 people and then finally get some wing-dings and hot fries and some Henny to chase it down with. While I'm waiting on my order I look over to my right and guess who I see?!

"Congratulations, Crystal," says Spin.

"Thank you," I try not to look surprised that she's there, but really I'm shocked.

"So when's the big day?!"

"I don't know yet, no time soon, you know I'll be busy!" I say nonchalantly. "What are you doing here Spin?" I finally ask. I can't hold it in any longer.

"I was driving and I heard it on the radio, an engagement party for Pops and Vanilla, blah, blah, blah! So I figured I'd come and see it with my own eyes. So you're really going to marry the nigga, huh?"

"Don't start the shit, Spin, not now, not here." I'm pissed now. "Where's Nikki by the way?"

"I just wanted to see you one more time, V, that's all!" She gets up and grabs her purse and keys, ready to leave, then she turns around and looks at me with tears in her eyes. "I still love you, you know!" She says, then turns away and walks out my life forever, breaking my heart in two. Damn I still love the girl!

But that shit is over with, Pops means the world to me now. Spin's going to have to go on. I turn around to see where the screaming is coming from and see Spin yelling at Pops, while he just stands there and looks at her and lets her get it off her chest, which I'm very grateful for.

"Spin, please leave!" I run up to her and grab her.

"I swear, V, I'm going to kill this nigga, you're still my motherfucking wife; you always will be! You don't love this nigga for real, please don't do this, I love you so much!"

She's crying like a baby now, looking so hurt, my heart is breaking.

"Spin, it's over, I *do* love him and I *will* marry him. It's over. It's been over for a minute, please move on with your life. If you need some money to get back on your feet, I'll give you some money, just please leave me alone!"

"I don't want your fucking money, V! Fuck you bitch! You think you can buy everything don't you?! That's your problem money is everything now! When we met you were as broke as hell and we were happy. Then you started making money off these hoes and me!" She points at Sophia and the girls and flips the script! "I hope the nigga fucks you over, Crystal, he's already fucking somebody you know, ask him!" She looks over at Pops. "Tell her you lying, no good bastard!"

"What is she talking about, Pops?" I'm pissed off and confused. "Sophia get my food and drink please!" I tell my girl.

"Alright!"

"She's crazy, V!" Pops replies, then turns and says, "Security, get this bitch out of here, she's ruining my engagement party!"

"Fuck you, Pops; it ain't over yet, bitch!" Spin screams at him and runs out the door.

"Come on, V, she wants you back baby, she's talking crazy, the hoe's lying!"

"Let's go home, Pops!" I say.

"Not yet baby, I've got some business to take care off first. Go and eat your food and kick it with your girls." He kisses me and walks away.

I turn around and see Sophia with my food and drink smiling at me.

"Come on, V, let's get drunk."

"Good idea!" I smile and we all walk over to the bar.

"Maybe it's good that she got it out of her system. Better now than later."

"You may be right, Sophia." I slam my drink and eat the food too fast, while I think about what Spin said, especially about Pops fucking somebody I know.

She was probably just talking crazy to get me back. I'm going to find out though. I hope it ain't true. I'll kill him.

Finally at 1:45am everybody starts to say their goodbyes, and by 2:30am, Pops and me are on the freeway going back to his house.

"Pops, why would she say some shit like that if it wasn't true, that ain't like Spin, trust me, I know her."

"Come on, V, don't start this shit now, we just got engaged a few hours ago, all the bitch was trying to do was ruin our engagement party, she just said the first thing that came to her mind. Who do you think I'm fucking that you know anyway?"

"Shit, you tell me?" I ask him seriously.

"You think I would fuck one of the hoes that work for you?"

"Would you, Terrell?"

"Girl, hell no, those hoes ain't even on my level! Don't come at me like that, V, you're pissing me the fuck off believing the hoe over me! I just asked you to marry me and you think I'm fucking somebody you know? If you think that then don't marry me!"

"Maybe I won't Pops!" I scream over the music and speed up.

"You'd better slow the fuck down, I've got dope in the trunk; you're going to get us pulled over and get us caught up in a dope case!" He yells at me, pissed.

"Well you could have told me you had shit in my car, Pops!"

"Oh, it's *your* car and *my* shit now, huh?"

"Well it's the truth ain't it?"

"You've got no problem spending *my* money though!"

"Fuck you and your money, Pops. I was fine without you and I will be fine now or whenever, with whoever! I don't need your fucking money!"

"V, please baby, I don't want to fight today or go to jail, please slow down and stop cursing and yelling at me, let's talk about this when we get home, alright?"

"Yeah, whatever," I say and turn up the radio.

We finally get to his house and I pull up in front and hit the brake, waiting for him to get out.

"What are you doing, Crystal? Pull into the driveway."

"I'm going to my house tonight, I need to be alone and think, please don't try to change my mind."

"What the hell have you got to think about?"

"You, us, everything!" I yell again. "Look, I'm not going to be yelling out here, just please go into the house, Pops, I'll call you tomorrow."

"Pop the trunk, Crystal," he says and gets out the car slamming the door behind him.

I pop the trunk and see him get a gym bag out, go up to the door, open it and throw the bag inside. He locks the door, gets in his car and tries to back out. I pull up in front of the driveway blocking him in and calling his phone.

"What the hell are you doing, Pops? Where are you going at 3:00am?"

"I've got business to take care of."

"You weren't thinking about your business a minute ago if I was about to go in the house!"

"Well you ain't, so I might as well take care of my business and make my money!" He's yelling at me now.

"You do what you want, Pops, because I will do what I want too!"

"What the fuck is that supposed to mean?"

"This is what it means!"

I put the car in park, get out and walk up to his car. I tell him to roll the window down. He does, looking confused. I take the ring off and throw it in his lap with a smile on my face and walk back towards the car and get in. Damn, that felt good! As soon as I close the door he jumps out and tries to open my car door, but it's locked. I laugh and pull off on his ass, laughing. About 10 seconds later my phone is ringing. I answer, and before he gets a chance to say anything I go off.

"It's over Pops; fuck you, your money and everything you stand for! I can't do this shit. I can't trust you. I can't and won't marry you!"

"Crystal, baby, I ain't going anywhere, please turn around and come back to the house. I was just going for a ride to clear my mind. I was trying to make you stay by acting like I was leaving. I didn't expect you to break off our engagement hours after we got engaged! Please baby, come back to the house!"

"Don't play mind games with me!"

"I'm sorry, please, V, come to the house, or I'll just follow you wherever you're going. We can drive around until we run out of gas!"

"I'll meet you back at the house, Pops" I say and hang up.

I guess I'll just find Spin tomorrow and ask her a few questions. Damn I love that man. I hope she's just talking crazy.

I get back in the house and Pops is sitting on the porch waiting for me, he beat me there by two minutes. I had to stop at the store for some cigarettes.

"Come here, Crystal, let's talk, baby." He says in his cool voice. I sit next to him lighting another cigarette, because I'm nervous.

"You need to quit smoking so much, V." He says looking serious.

"You're the reason I'm smoking twice as much as I used to."

"Don't blame it on me now, because you're the one that let the bull crap affect you. All the shit Spin said is nothing but lies. She's saying shit to get back at you. The hoe can't stand the fact we're getting married."

"So, you don't mind if I ask her who she was talking about then." I say, looking serious as hell and blowing the smoke up in the air. I look up to the sky, while I feel Pops' eyes staring at me.

"She wasn't talking about anybody, because there isn't anybody! You believe her over me, huh?"

"I just want to ask her why she said it then, if there ain't anybody then you shouldn't mind if I ask her!" I get up, fling my cig butt on the ground and go into the house.

Pops comes in right after me.

"I don't want you talking to the bitch at all, Crystal!" He looks mad and serious as hell.

"Why? Have you got something to hide?"

"Hell no, I just don't want your ex around you; she's already started enough shit as it is!" He's screaming now.

"How would you like it if I went and saw my ex?"

"You've got no reason to see her!" I yell back.

"You've got no reason to see that hoe either!" He's up in my face now.

"Go ahead Pops, hit me!" I'm pissed as hell now. "You know you want to! Why do I even bother with your punk ass?! You ain't all that."

Smack! He slaps the shit out of me.

"Don't even test me again, V!" He leaves and slams the door. I lock it behind him and hear him pull off. I've got to leave this A.S.A.P!

About two minutes later, his house phone rings. I answer it.

"Hello?" I say with a weak voice.

"Baby, I love you, I want you to be my wife. I don't want to hurt you, but you don't listen worth a shit! I ain't one of your hoes; you can't tell me what to do, Crystal! I wear the pants in this relationship and you're going to show me a little more respect from now on. And don't even try to act like you're going to break up with me, because that ain't happening over my dead body! I'll be home in the morning. You'd better be there, and if I was you, I wouldn't even try to call Spin if you don't want anything to happen to her! Have you got all of that, Ma?"

"Have you lost your motherfucking mind, Pops?"

"No, I'm just telling you like it is, that's all!"

"Over my dead body, Pops!" I hang up and grab my keys.

I pop my trunk, open the back doors, go up stairs and bring down the bags I packed the night before. I throw them in the car. I'm out of here! This man is crazy I'm going to my mother's for tonight.

Chapter 13:

It's 9:45am and my cell-phone is blowing up. It's Pops, and he's already left eight messages, talking crazy and shit. I finally answer.

"What do you want?" I say like he's slow.

"You'd better get your shit together and come back to the house in the next few hours, Crystal!"

"Or what, Pops?"

"You don't want to know what will happen next. Just do as I say and everything is going to be alright."

"You've got problems, Pops. You've really lost it. Can't you see that I don't want your ass anymore?"

"It's not what you want, V, it's what you're going to do if you don't want shit happening to your family."

He hangs up. I get in the shower, get dressed, and call Sophia. I transfer my calls, say bye to my mom, and go back to Pops' house. The bitch and me have got some shit to talk about. He's just fucked up trying to threaten my family. I get out of the car and practically run up to the door. I open it and go in. Pops is on the couch with Kevin and Dru, watching the game.

"Hey baby, you finally got here I see." He walks up to me and kisses my cheek like nothing happened, then, seeing the look of shock in my eyes, he whispers in my ear, "Don't even think about it." I just walk away and go upstairs.

"Damn, what's wrong with her, Pops?"

"She's mad at one of her hoes or something" I hear him say, then they all laugh and continue watching the game and talking about other things.

I get upstairs, look at the dresser and see the ring on it. I leave it there. I can't believe him; I hate him so much right now. I've got to do something about this. I'll just have to play along with his little plan until I figure out how to get rid of this man without anybody getting hurt. I look at the ring again, grab it and put it on. I re-apply my makeup and go back downstairs like nothing happened.

"Baby, have you seen my 2-way?" I ask him so nicely.

"No, where'd you have it last?"

"I thought it was in your car, the Jag."

"I ain't seen it, Mami." He's looking at me funny, probably trying to figure out why I'm being nice.

"Let me see the rock, V?" Kevin asks me smiling.

I run over like a little girl, waving my hand in front of him, smiling hard. I glance over at Pops, he just looks confused, but he acts cool.

"Damn girl, your shit's worth about a mill ticket!" Kevin is playing around.

"My baby deserves the best!" Pops says and pulls me close to him, making me sit on his lap.

I smile, lean over, and kiss his forehead. Then I get back up, telling him I've got to run to the store.

"I'll go with you baby, it's dark."

"I'm straight, Boo, this ain't the hood. Do you think one of these old white folks is going to rob me?"

"Shit, you never know!" He says, smiling.

"I'll get whatever you need, ma, don't leave the boys here by themselves."

"They're family, they're tight!"

"Alright then, come on. Kev, do you want something from the store?"

"No, I'm tight."

Damn, I don't want this bitch going with me. I leave the house and get in the car. Pops follows me, smiling.

"Say, you've come to your senses I see?"

"Just leave my family out of this, Terrell!" I look at him serious as hell with so much hate in my eyes. I know he can feel it.

"Stop looking at me like that, V."

"Like what? Like I despise the ground you walk on? The air you breathe? Well, guess what, I do! I really hate you, Pops. I hope you're happy!" I stop at the store and get out.

I get what I need and get back in the car. He never even got out of the car.

"V, baby, I'm sorry for snapping like that, but you don't understand, I've never loved anybody like I love you, I can't just let you go, it ain't going to happen. Just relax and everything will work out just fine." He reaches over to kiss me, but I pull back. "You'd better stop pulling back too; you ain't going to put me through this shit. Like it or not you ain't going anywhere, you got that?" He grabs my face and kisses my lips.

"Yeah, Pops, I'll fake this whole relationship for you if that's what you want."

"I don't want you to fake it. Why can't you just act like you did when we first met, Crystal?"

"Because it's going to be fake, Pops, that's why! You didn't hit me then, and you didn't lie to me, or beat me like I'm a man, or cheat on me, or threaten my family! That's why!" I pull in in-front of the house, turn the car off and get out.

"V!" He yells out the window.

"Yes?" I say, faking a smile. I turn around and go straight into the house.

"Are you alright, V?" Kevin asks me.

"Yeah, I'm fine!" I snap and run upstairs, hitting the bed and crying.

I hate this bitch so much! There's only one way to do this. About fifteen minutes later he comes up and pats me on my shoulder.

"What, Pops? Please, I need to get some sleep."

"Baby, let's make this shit work, okay?"

"Just let me be, please. Why don't you just leave me the hell alone?"

"You know too much about my business, V, I can't just let you go and shit, are you crazy?"

"I ain't going to tell anybody about your business, you know I ain't a snitch!"

"Sorry baby, but I can't take the chance." He walks out of the room and closes the door.

I get on the phone and call Sophia to check up on everything. I call my Mom's to make sure everything's is alright, and then finally I fall asleep.

***

Before I know it, it's 9:30am and the alarm clock is going off. I jump up and lie there for a minute. Finally I get up, jump in the shower, and do all my morning things. I go downstairs and see that Pops is passed out on the couch with an empty bottle of Henny beside him. I remember him saying last night that he had to do something by 11:00am, so I shake him to wake him up.

He jumps like crazy, and then looks at me and smiles.

"Good morning, Mami. What time is it?"

"It's 10:15am. Don't you have somewhere to be by 11:00am? I thought I heard you say that last night."

"Oh shit, I've got to meet my dog and take care of some business, do you want to come?"

"No, that's alright, I've got to check on the girls and go to the bank. Then I've got to go and see my Mom. I'll see you later." I start heading for the door.

"Crystal!"

"Yeah?"

"I love you, baby."

"Yeah," I walk out the house, disgusted.

I get in the caddy and hit the E way on my way to the room to see Sophia and to pick up my drops. I've got to go halla at my girls today. Nobody really knows what's going on, but I've got to tell *somebody* just in case this crazy ass fool does something to me before I get a chance to do what I've got to do.

"Landy?"

"Hey, girl, what's up, are you busy?"

"We've got to meet, it's important."

"What's wrong?"

"I can't talk about this over the phone; I'm on my way to pick you up. I'll tell you in the car on our way to see Sophia and pick up my drops."

"Alright, I'll see you in a minute."

"Bye."

About twenty minutes later I pull up in front of my girl's house. She takes her sweet time to come out, like always.

"Damn bitch, finally!"

"Shut up! What's up?"

"Girl, I've got a problem that's out of this world."

"Is one of your hoes acting up?"

"I wish it was that easy. It's Pops. The man went crazy. He's flipped the script for real!"

"What did he do?" She sounds surprised.

"Girl, the bitch hit me, threatened my family, and he's fucking around too! I suppose he comes and goes when he wants, calls me all kinds of bitches and hoes."

"Why don't you leave his ass?" She makes it sound so easy.

"He won't let me!" I snap. "He threatens my family and talks all kinds of crazy shit about how he loves me too much, and I know too much of his business. He says he can't take the chance of letting me go. He puts on this big-ass front in front of people, and then flips the script when we are alone. I swear he's bipolar or something."

"What are you going to do? When did this shit start?"

"Girl, the night he asked me to marry him."

"Hell no!"

"Hell yeah! I've got a plan for his ass. I'm going to play it cool for a minute. I just wanted to tell you in case something happens to me or my family. I want somebody to know. Don't say a word to anybody though, for real."

"Girl, you know I won't. Just be careful, and don't do anything stupid!"

"I won't, trust me!"

We finally pull up in front of the hotel. I tell Landy to wait a minute while I go up and halla at Sophia.

"Hey, baby girl!" I walk over to her and give her a hug and a kiss.

"I miss you, Sophie!"

"You've been acting all antisocial since you got you a boyfriend and shit!"

"It ain't like that girl, we just moved in together, so we are spending time together and seeing how this is going to work out. You know this living together and shit."

"Have you talked to Spin?" She drops the bomb on me like it's nothing.

"No, I don't want to!" I say really loud and stern.

"You don't want to know what she was trying to say the night at the club?"

"The bitch is probably lying anyway. You know she's mad as hell about me leaving her ass for Pops."

"I don't know. Spin knows something if you ask me."

"Well, whatever the slut knows, I don't want to know!" I say sarcastically.

"It's your man!"

"Right, it is, you worry about yours! Oops, you don't have one! Ha-ha!"

"Funny bitch," Sophie slaps my arm playfully.

"Look though, I've got to bounce! Landy is waiting in the car, I've got to drop her off and go halla at the other hoes, you feeling me?"

"Alright baby girl, love you!"

"Love you too."

"Call me."

"I will."

I go back to the car. Landy is on the phone talking to somebody.

"Where are we going now?" She asks.

"I've got to go halla at Suhey and Diamond and get my drops. Sophia picked the rest of them up for me, so I've got it here!"

"Come on then, let's go."

"Are you hanging with me for the day?"

"For sure! Let's go to the liquor store!"

"Now you're talking." I laugh and pull out of the parking lot.

Once I do what I've got to do far as my money goes, I make a quick stop at my parent's house, halla at them for a minute and then bounce to the park. Messing around with Landy, I'm already drunk and ready to hit the park and act a fool.

"I'm about to call Spin and see what the hell she was talking about the other night at the club."

"What are you talking about?" Landy asks, confused.

"Remember when she said that Pops was fucking somebody I know?"

"Yeah, but don't you think she was just talking crazy?"

"No, not Spin, she knows something and I'm about to find out."

I dial her number on my phone.

"Hey Spin" I say after she answers, sounding like she's asleep.

"Vanilla?"

"Yeah, it's me. Look I know you probably don't want to talk to me, but I need to know what you were talking about in the club on the night of my engagement."

"You call me for this bullshit now? You didn't want to hear me then! What, you finally found out that your prince charming isn't who he seemed to be?"

"Something like that. Can you please tell me what you were talking about?"

"I'm going to say one word, Crystal, you figure out the rest."

"Say it already!" I yell over the phone.

"Arizona." She says and hangs up.

"What?" She's gone by the time I can get the word out.

"What did she say?" Landy asks me.

"She said, 'Arizona'."

"What's that supposed to mean?"

"It can only mean one thing."

I call Sophia.

"Sophia, where is Ebony working at?"

"She's on 12 mile and Tele, why?"

"Don't book the bitch anymore!"

"What's wrong?"

"I'll tell you later, I've got to go, what room number is she in?"

"134. What's up, V?"

"You'll see in a minute."

About fifteen minutes later, after flying 90 on the freeway and using every cuss word in the book and inventing some new ones along the way, I pull up in front of the Red Roof Inn. I tell Landy to stay in the car. I leave it running and open the back door wide open. Landy is still trying to calm me down, asking me not to do anything stupid.

I go to room 134 and knock on the door. Ebony opens it, smiling. The fake ass bitch! I walk in, grab the hoe by her hair and throw her against the wall.

"So you think you can get away with fucking Pops, huh, bitch?"

"Vanilla, please, let me explain!"

"Explain what, Ebony? I made you, bitch, and this how you repay me?" I look shocked for a minute, and then I come back to my senses and back off long enough to hear her out.

"Talk to me, Ebony," I say with a calm voice.

"He threatened me with everything possible, saying me he was going to tell you I tried to fuck him, and that it would be over for me far as working for you. He said all kinds of crazy shit! The nigga even slapped me, V."

"Chill out! I'm sorry," I snap. "I believe you, I don't believe him. I told you and everybody else from the beginning that you work for me, not the nigga, he doesn't run shit!"

"I don't know how he acts towards you, but he's crazy to me, V!"

She won't stop crying. I walk over to her and hug her and ask her to stop crying.

"Come on, get cleaned up and come have a drink with me and my girl, Landy."

"Are you sure?"

"Positive. Don't worry about him, I've got this. I promise he won't get away with this. Let me call Sophia and tell her you're going to be off for the day! I did fire you before I got here, but you're hired again!" I smile and call Sophia and tell her the deal.

"Let's roll," I say to Ebony after I get off the phone.

"One more thing, before we leave, don't breathe a word of this to anybody, do you understand?"

"Trust me, I won't! I was scared to tell you!"

"You should have been," I smile and walk out the door, Ebony follows behind me.

"Is everything alright, V?" Landy asks me, looking confused.

"Yeah, everything's cool. That coward, Pops, has been playing mind games with people, but I've got something for the bitch."

I put Trina in and bump my shit loud as hell on our way to the Isle. My phone rings while I'm parked at the Isle, just kicking back, drinking, and watching some young cats break-dancing. I look at my caller ID, it's Pops. I decide to play it cool and answer it.

"What's up, doe?" I say, laughing.

"Where are you at?"

"At the Isle with my girls, what's up?"

"When are you coming home?"

"I'm not sure, why?"

"Be here tonight, Crystal!"

"I will, Pops, bye!" I hang up before he says anything else.

Damn I hate the man. I'm not going to let him ruin my day.

"Was that him?" Landy asks me.

"Yeah, he wants me to come home tonight" I say, rolling my eyes.

"Ebony, would you excuse us, please?" I ask her to leave the car.

She nods and gets out.

"Yeah, I've got to play it cool until I get rid of him." I tell Landy.

"V, what do you mean until you 'get rid of him'?"

"Just what I said; I'm going to end this shit soon, Landy. All I need is proof that this bitch is threatening me and my family and that shouldn't be that hard since he repeats that shit to me all day long; every time I try to do anything he doesn't like."

"Are you going to set him up or something?"

"Something like that, but way deeper." I smirk and gesture for Ebony to get back in the car.

Once she's in, I pull out on my way to drop them off. I've got shit to take care of.

"Alright girl, I'll call you when I get in tonight" I tell Ebony when I drop her off at the hotel.

"Be careful, V."

"I'll be alright, girl, you take it easy and make some money!" I smile and pull off.

"You just don't stop, do you?" Landy tells me, laughing.

"Shit doesn't stop because I've got a little problem; I've still got to make my money."

"Right, right," she laughs. "Let me guess, you're about to go there now?"

"I'm going to hit the mall for a second, and then go and see him."

"Alright, just call me when you get in."

"You know I will." I turn the radio up and we ride without saying a word to each other for the next fifteen minutes until I get to her house.

"I'll halla at you once I hit the crib, alright?"

"Don't do anything stupid, V" Landy tells me and closes the door.

"Oh, I will" I say to myself as I pull off.

I've got to hit the mall and go to Radioshack to get a tape recorder so I can tape everything the bitch has got to say to me from now on. Nothing and nobody is going to mess this up for me. Nobody.

On my way to the car as I leave *Northland Mall*, I pull out the little tape recorder I bought and try it again, making sure it works, of course it does. But what the hell am I going to do with this? I think to myself. I have a feeling it's going to be useful sometime soon. I get in the car, put in some Usher and go to see this so-called man of mine.

Chapter 14:

I pull up in front of Pops' house, get out of the car, lock the door, and put the tape recorder in my purse. I keep my purse open so it will be able to record clearly. He's never gone through my shit before; let's hope he doesn't do it now.

I walk in the house and see him sitting on the couch watching MTV and hanging up the phone. It was probably one of his hoes.

"Hey baby," he says smiling at me.

"Hey, what's up?"

"You tell me, beautiful." He walks up to me and kisses my lips.

I wonder which one of his hoes he's been kissing today.

"One of my girls quit today." I say, as cool as I can.

"Oh yeah, which one?"

"Ebony, the chick from Arizona. I went to pick up my drop and she had her suitcases packed and she asked me if I could take her to the airport. Since I was coming this way anyway, I did. She just said she was tired and wanted to go back home. She was cool, I liked her, but I guess she just didn't want to hoe no more." I laugh and look at him. He looks pissed.

"What are you looking like that for?"

"That's all she said?" He asks looking scared and shit.

"Yeah, what else was she supposed to say?"

"You're just going to let the hoe leave like that?"

"There's plenty more where she came from! Why do you look all mad about it?" I ask him.

"I ain't mad about that shit. I've got some other shit on my mind, that's all. How was the park?" He's trying to change the subject.

"Boring," I say, hitting a square and going upstairs, hoping he doesn't follow me.

Thank God he doesn't.

I make my calls to Landy and Ebony to let them know I'm back at the house, and then I hit the hay.

***

I wake up in the middle of the night, and go downstairs to get some water. It's 4:17am on the clock. Damn my head is banging from drinking too much, and I'm thirsty as hell. I try to be quiet so I won't wake Pops up.

He must have fallen asleep on the couch, because he never came up to bed, but once I get downstairs I realise that he ain't there, so I check the guest room. He's not there either. In a way I'm happy, he's probably out with one of his hoes. Good, at least it's somebody other than me. I don't want to see the bitch any more than I have to. Yes, that's his new name now.

I look on the kitchen table, there's a note from Pops saying, "Baby, I'll be back tomorrow night. I had a call and had to make a really quick run to Chicago, I didn't want to wake you. Here's some money, go and buy you something cute from me. I love you, Pops."

"I hate that bitch." I say to myself.

I throw the note in the garbage, grab the money and take it upstairs and put it in my purse. The bitch really thinks he can buy me.

I go back downstairs and rewind the tape I hid in the dresser by the phone to see if I can find out where he really went. I'm going to have a lot of fun with this recording shit. I fast forward the tape. I hear the phone ringing and Pops picking it up. Too bad I can only hear a one way conversation.

"Yeah," he answers, the T.V. is on in the background.

"Right now, dog? I've got the shit, but can't you wait until tomorrow?"

"Well, if I leave right now I can be there in five hours or so."

"Since you got all the cheese, I'll be there, alright, dog." He hangs up and goes out the back door to the garage; I suppose to get the dope. Then he comes back in. I can hear him grabbing the keys, turning the T.V. off, and leaving like two minutes later, probably right after writing the note.

"Well, I guess the bitch was telling the truth for once." I say out loud and erase the tape and put it back where it was. I go back upstairs and set the alarm clock for 10:00am, and then I fall asleep.

The alarm goes off before I know it. It takes me about twenty minutes to get out of bed, but finally I do. I get in the shower, throw on some shorts, a tank top, and sandals, and put my hair up in a ponytail. I put on a baseball cap, a touch of lip gloss, and some Gucci perfume, before grabbing my purse, phone, keys and hitting the streets by 11:15am.

I make all my necessary calls. Sophia has got everything under control, money is flowing in well, everything is groovy; except, of course, Pops. And that's one big problem I'm going to have to deal with soon. I've got to get into his cars to put bugs in there too. I want to know everything the bitch is doing.

I've got to call my boy Chill and find out how to bug the phone. I doubt I can get hold of his cell-phone long enough to do it, but at least I can do the house phone. I'm going to go and see my family today, and take my nephew to the park, or the mall, or wherever he wants to go.

But before I do anything I've got to call Spin and thank her; I owe her the biggest apology. Sometimes I wonder what my life would have been if I had never met Pops. Me and Spin would probably still be together. She wouldn't be with Nikki, that's for sure. I wonder if they are still messing around. I hope not. Damn, what am I doing? Why am I even thinking about Spin like that? Why do I care if she's with Nikki, or anybody for that matter? But deep down I do. I still love her. I think I always will. And deep in my heart, I believe she still loves me. I hurt her so badly, and all over a good-for-nothing man. God I hope she will forgive me, or at least talk to me. I know she will never take me back; I wouldn't either after all the shit I put her through. I want her to be my friend at least, hell, I want her to talk to me at least.

I dial her number. She picks up after four and a half rings, sounding sleepy.

"Hello, Spin?"

"Yeah, who's this?" She asks with the sexy sleepy voice I miss so much.

"This is Crystal, can you talk?" I sound nervous as hell.

"What!" She snaps. "What the hell do you want to talk to me about? I don't have time for this shit, Crystal. Bye!"

"Please don't hang up, baby, I'm sorry, I miss you! I love you, and I know I messed up. I hate this man, I need you. Just meet me so we can talk, please I'm begging you!"

"Hell no," she starts laughing. "You expect me to say okay, I forgive you, let's try this again baby? Hell no, Vanilla. Bitch, you put me through hell over a nigga who fucks everybody on the planet. He's probably given you some shit by now, and you just think you can say you're sorry and I'm supposed to say 'okay'?!"

"No baby, I don't, just please meet me, I've got a lot to tell you. I don't trust anybody, Spin. A lot of shit is going on. I need you, please, just talk to me! Can I come over?" I can't believe I'm saying all of this.

"Yeah, come on, this better be good! But don't think I'm going to jump back into your arms, Crystal!"

"I don't baby. I deserve whatever you throw my way. I'll be there in fifteen minutes. I do love you Spin."

"Bye, Vanilla," she hangs up.

"I guess I deserved that." I say to myself. I want my baby back and I will do whatever it takes. It might take a minute, but I *will* get my wife back. I look at the ring on my finger that Pops gave me. I take it off and throw it out the window. He'll probably beat my ass for it, but fuck it; I don't want anything that reminds me of that bitch. The way he has been acting, he probably won't even notice now. I haven't worn it anyway.

I finally pull up in front of Spin's apartment, park the car, get out, and walk to the door. I'm about to knock right when she opens the door, looking beautiful with tears in her eyes.

"Come in," she says and I do without saying a word.

God help me through this! She closes the door.

"Do you want a drink?" She asks me really calm. It's kind of scary.

"Yeah, have you got a beer?"

It may sound stupid but I don't want her to make me a drink; God only knows what she might to do to it. I could use a shot of Henny right about now though.

"Yeah, do you want a MGD or a Corona?"

"MGD will do," I say, still standing by the doorway.

"You can sit down; I ain't going to do anything to you." She laughs and goes into the kitchen to get the beer.

She comes back with two of them and a bottle opener. She pops them in front of me. I'm glad because then I know she hasn't put shit in it.

"Thank you, Spin," I say looking at her. Damn she still looks good as hell, even better. She's a little thicker, but all in the right places. I snap out of it when she asks why it is so important that we talk in person.

"Everything Spin, us, life, my family. I'm scared and confused, that bitch, Pops, is crazy. I wish I had never fucked around with him. I wish I had never lost you over this bullshit. It's bad enough I lost you. But now I'm worried about what that bitch is going to do to my family if I leave. And I am going to leave, one way or another. And the way shit is looking it's going to be ugly when I do." I blurt out. "I've got tape recorders all through the house, and in two of his cars. I've even bugged the house phone, just so I can have enough evidence to nail him if he tries to hurt me or my family. I'm ready to kill him, Spin. This shit is getting out of control."

"Crystal, slow down. Don't tell me you came here to ask me to help you get rid of Pops. That ain't going to happen. I don't want anything to do with it. You deserve everything you've got coming to you far as I'm concerned." She smirks at me.

"You know what, Spin, *I* may deserve it, but my family doesn't. That's what he is after and I'm not going to let that happen. Over my dead body!" I get up and storm out of the apartment crying like a baby.

I have never been afraid in my life like I am right now. The thought of him even touching my family makes my blood boil with anger. I know what I've got to do before he gets the chance to do it to me. There's going to be some blood spilt, but it's not going to be mine or my family's.

Chapter 15:

I pull up in front of his house, feeling a little better; maybe because my mind is made up regardless of what the consequences may be. I don't care what happens as long as my family is safe. Hopefully I will be also.

I get in the house and check the answering machine. Pops' Mom called, as well as his cousin, his sister, and two of his homeboys. They are all saying that they called his cell-phone and he is not answering, so they thought he might be at home. I check my phone too. I see that his Mom called me while I was at Spin's, but I had my phone turned off. She left me a message asking me to call her if I'm with Pops, or as soon as I hear from him.

I check the rest of my messages, call a few people back, then try to call Pops myself. It's not like him not to answer the phone when his Mama calls. Hell, he even answered her calls while we were having sex! His answer machine comes on. I leave a brief message and tell him to call me at home if he gets the message in the next few hours, if not, call my cell-phone. I hang up, go upstairs and take a nap. I've got shit to put together, I need some rest.

I wake up about four hours later. Pops is still gone, but he will probably be back in the next few hours; it's almost night time. I check my phone, his Mama called again and Spin. I hurry up and dial Spin's number. She answers on the second ring.

"You called me?" I say, surprised.

"Yeah, I was a little rough on you because I was so mad at you, and it wasn't even you that you came to see me about, it was your family. I still love them and I miss them too."

"You can see them any time you want, Spin, you know that." I cut her off.

"I think it's better if I don't, so I won't miss them anymore."

"Spin, do you love me?" I say with as much confidence as I can.

"I don't want to talk about that, Crystal."

"I do. Everybody makes mistakes; I'm not perfect. It's just that some fuck up more than others. *I* fucked up more than others, but everybody deserves a chance to at least explain themselves."

"There's nothing you can say that will change my mind, Vanilla. I still care for you, but there's nothing in this world you can possibly do to win back my trust and respect for you! I used to worship the ground you walked on, but after the night you got engaged that shit ended. You believed that nigga over me! After all these years, I tell you he is fucking somebody else and you think I'm lying or something! What, did you think I was hating?" she laughs. "You had to find out for yourself, the ugly way, that your hubby was fucking one of your hoes. Where is she anyway?"

I quickly think of something to say.

"I sent her back to Arizona; she wanted to leave."

"You know why, right? He was threatening her and basically raping her! The girl was scared to death."

"How do you know her anyway?" I ask out of curiosity.

"I grew up with her cousin. Pops dropped her off one day and she came into the house looking scared as hell. We asked her what was wrong, but she wouldn't tell us. My girl, her cousin, told me that she had been working for some escort service when she got here. She said that a female ran it, so I knew it was you. I went upstairs and kicked it with her and put two and two together. But before that, I heard enough shit about Pops in the hood. Once we split, everybody had something to say about you and him, or just about how he rolls."

"Thank you for everything, Spin, I'm sorry I ever hurt you and I'm sorry I ever stopped trusting you. I'm so sorry I messed up what we had. I can't do shit over, even if I tried, all I can do is apologise and ask for another chance."

"Crystal, I'm sorry but I can't do it, it's over. I hope you move on and find someone that will make you happy, a woman or a man. I do wish you the best. I've got to go. Bye, Crystal." She hangs up.

I hold the phone for a few more seconds before I hang up and dial Pops' Mom's house. She answers on the second ring. Before I get to say a word, she speaks first.

"Let me talk to the boy, he could have at least called me back!" She sounds mad.

"I'm sorry, Mrs Hardgrove, but he's not here and he hasn't called me all day or answered his phone or returned anybody's calls. All I got was a note he left saying he'd be back tonight, but I have no idea what time. Maybe something is wrong with his phone?"

"It better be good. I hope he hasn't got himself in trouble. Do me a favour and call the jail, would you?" She sounds serious.

"I know he went to Chicago, so he is not in jail here. If it will make you feel better, I will call Indiana and Chicago to see if he's there. I hope not, though."

"Okay baby, call me back and let me know what they say."

"I will Mrs Hardgrove, but let's give him until tonight to get home, okay? I'm going to be here in case he calls."

"Alright baby, take care of yourself."

"Goodnight, Mrs Hardgrove. You get some sleep." I hang up, feeling like something ain't right.

I take the tape recorder out of the kitchen house phone, and do the same to both cars. Something's not right and I don't want any part of it. It's not what I planned, and I will not pay for somebody else's mistakes. I have a funny feeling he's got himself in trouble. Maybe he *is* in jail. I'll give him until 12:00am to call, if not, I'm calling Chi town and Indiana to see if he's there.

I finally go upstairs and set the alarm clock for 12:00am. I go and take a nice hot shower, give myself a facial mask, and make a few phone calls. I tell Sophia to drop my money off tomorrow morning at my house.

"Put it in the mail box if I'm not here, but only after 11:30am, after the mail runs." I tell her. All I need is the mail man taking my money.

I would tell her to come here, but Pops is really funny about me bringing my girls to the house.

Finally I lie down and decide to take a nap until 12:00am. If Pops doesn't call by then, I'm calling the Police station.

***

The alarm clock goes off. I check the messages on my phone, Pops still hasn't called. I call information and get the number for the Chicago and Indiana Police Stations. I call Indiana first, nothing. So I finally decide to call Chicago. I know he is on the south side somewhere. I remember him saying a while back that he deals with some cats off 79th and Stony Island. Someone finally answers.

"Hello, I'm calling to check if you have someone in custody?"

"The name...?" An officer asks, sounding irritated.

"Terrell Hardgrove, he's from Michigan."

"Hold on a minute."

I get put on hold. About three minutes later she gets back on the phone.

"Yes, we had him, but he's in the hospital right now, he was shot six times."

"What?!" I scream, shocked.

I almost drop the phone.

"Do you want the number of the hospital he's in?"

"Yeah, please."

I look for pen and paper and write down the number. I say a quick thank you and hang up. I call the hospital immediately.

"I'm calling to check on the status of Terrell Hardgrove, he's been shot." My voice is shaky.

 I'm ready to cry, but I don't for some weird reason. I'm kind of happy. Shocked, but happy. The bitch deserves everything that comes his way.

"Hold on a minute, please." This time they put me on hold for like fifteen minutes, which seems like fifteen hours!

I call Pops' Mom on my cell-phone and fill her in on what's going on. She's freaking out. She starts screaming and crying, which finally makes me shed some tears, but only because I feel her pain as a mother. That is her baby, her only son. No matter how much I hate him; to her he can do no wrong. She's asking me 101 questions that I don't have the answers to.

Finally someone gets on the phone, I tell Mrs Hardgrove to hold on.

"Who are you waiting for?" A nurse asks me.

I'm getting aggravated now.

"I called to check on the status of Terrell Hardgrove, I've been on hold for twenty minutes. He's been shot six times, he's from Michigan."

"Oh, yeah, I just left his room, he's in a coma and, I'm sorry to tell you this, but so far the coma is irreversible."

"When can I see him?"

"Are you his kin?"

"Yes, I'm his wife." I can't believe I just said that.

"Whenever you get here then. I'm sorry, Mrs Hardgrove, we did everything we could."

"I'll be there on the next flight. I'm coming from Detroit, Michigan."

"Sure," She says and hangs up the phone.

I pick my cell-phone up. Pops' Mom is still on the phone, crying. I can hear a lot of people in the background; she's called everybody and their Mama.

"Mrs Hardgrove, he's in a coma. I'm on my way there. It's probably better if you don't go right now. He's in a coma so you won't be able to talk to him anyway. I'll call you as soon as I get there, okay? Please try to get some sleep." I leave out the part about him not coming out of it.

I pack my carry on, grab my passport and hit the road. I call Landy and tell her what happened. I ask her to meet me at my house because I don't want to fly down there by myself. I pull up in front of my house, she's already there. She gets out, gets in the car and hugs me.

"Are you alright?" She asks me.

I smile at her and say, "Everything is going to be alright in a minute."

"Do you think he's going to make it?" She asks me, not looking surprised at the fact that I'm not crying.

"If he does he's going to be a vegetable from what the doctors tell me, and I doubt his Mom is going to want him living like that."

Finally my life is going to be back in order! I hit the road and smile. She just shakes her head and says something that sounds like music to my ears.

"At least you don't have to do the dirty work."

"I sure don't, God doesn't like ugly! The bastard had it coming."

I turn up the music and watch her lay back all the way to the airport. It takes us about 30 minutes to get to the airport. When we arrive, we park the car. It's a slow night so we get our tickets right away and are on the next flight out. Before we know it, we're there.

Chapter 16:

The hospital is close to the airport; at least that's one good thing.

"Do you want me to go in with you too?" Landy asks.

"Shit, he can't talk anyway, so why not? I'd feel more comfortable with you there."

"Alright, hold up," she gets out and we walk to the hospital door.

I'm so nervous, but I'm trying not to show it. I'm not sure why, it's not like he can do anything to me now, unless you consider being a vegetable for life doing something! We walk into the hospital. I go straight to the bathroom. A few minutes later I come out. We walk up to the reception desk and ask the lady behind it what room Terrell Hardgrove is in. She shows us to room 12. I thank her and open the door to his hospital room.

My heart drops as I look at this sorry-ass bitch hooked up to a life support machine, looking helpless. He can't talk, move, or do anything else to hurt me ever again. Landy is just staring at him. I tell her to stop looking like that.

"Shit, he can't see or hear me anyway!"

"Shit, knowing him, you never know!" I tell her, and we both start laughing. I've got to call his Mama and let her know that we are here. I get on the phone and call her. She's crying again. I feel for her. As much as I want him dead, it is her baby.

"She's going to be here tomorrow morning." I tell Landy. "Let's go and get a room close by and hit one of these local bars tonight to celebrate this bastard's death." I say, smiling, while squeezing his hand. For a second, I could have sworn he squeezed it back. I jump back. Landy looks at me like I'm crazy. I start laughing and tell her I'm playing with her.

We leave the hospital and I try my hardest not to look nervous about what just happened in there. I hope I was only imagining his hand moving. I get in the car and pull out, trying not to think about it while we pull in at the Best Western. We go in and get a room. No matter how hard I try, I just can't get it out of my mind. I just know in my heart that he heard every word we said. I guess it really doesn't matter if he can hear as long as he can't talk or move. Pretty soon the plug is going to be pulled anyway.

We get to the room. I lock the door and turn the shower on. Landy tells me to hurry up so she can get in too. Within the next hour we are out the door and in the parking lot of some bar that is just around the corner from the hospital. We go in, order our drinks and have a ball. We dance with every fine Chi-town man, and flirt with every sexy female in the bar, trying to pick up a hoe to take back with me to the "D". Well, I am, Landy ain't trying to pick up anything but some new dick.

No matter how many fine women I meet, the only one I can think about is Spin. I've got to call her tomorrow. I need to see her. I need to get my baby back. We would still be together if this no-good man never came into my life. Thank God he will be leaving it any day now! I put Spin out of my mind for a minute and try to enjoy myself. I don't want to get too drunk since I've got to meet Pops' Mom at the hospital in the morning and make sure the plug gets pulled.

By 2:30am we're back at the room, ready to hit the sheets. I'm really not in the mood for company and I really don't feel like having to throw someone out early in the morning before Pops' Mom shows up.

Landy gets another room with some cat she met at the bar, so I'm alone and happy about it! Finally I can get some rest!

My alarm clock goes off at 8:00am. I get out of bed by 8:15am. I drink some water and pop four Tylenols to make sure I don't have a headache. I take a quick shower.

By 9:00am I'm ready to go downstairs and wait for his Mom to meet me in the lobby. Damn, I almost forgot about Landy!

"Landy, put the bitch out and come down here so I don't have to be with this woman by myself." I tell her when she answers her cell-phone.

"Oh shit, what time is it? Why didn't you call me when you got up?" She asks still sounding half drunk.

"Shit, to be honest, I forgot about you" I tell her seriously, but laughing.

"Fuck you, Crystal, I'll be down there in about thirty minutes." She hangs up the phone.

I walk over to the bar and order some breakfast for both of us, especially some coffee for me. Finally at 9:45am I see Landy coming down the stairs with some guy who still looks drunk. She gives him a halfway hug and tells him she'll call him. I just laugh while she sits down and starts killing her cold breakfast.

"Did you have fun?" I ask her.

"Yeah, it was alright." She answers with her mouth full.

"What's his name?"

"Hold on, let me see," she pulls a piece of paper out of her purse and reads it. "Dwayne," she says, then tosses the paper into the ashtray next to her.

"You're no good Landy."

"Nobody is going to drive four hours for some dick."

"I know that's right," I laugh, then look over my shoulder and see Pops' Mom come in the door.

"Shit, act depressed, she's here!" I whisper to her.

"Hey Mama, over here," I call out to her with the saddest face I can make.

"Hey, Crystal, let's go see my baby; I can't take this any longer."

"Please don't cry, Mama. I've been crying all night. I haven't slept. I just barely ate something. I was at the hospital all day until the nurse told us to leave."

"He loved you very much, baby," she tells me, and puts her head on my shoulder. She starts sobbing uncontrollably while I try to calm her down and walk her to the hospital. Landy is following behind us, not saying a word.

In about two minutes we're in the hospital and walking into Pops' room. The doctor tells us his condition is the same and there is virtually no chance that he will ever live without the life support machine and that it's up to me to pull the plug since I'm the beneficiary on his life insurance policy.

"I'm what?" I ask, shocked.

"Well, when the Police brought Mr Hardgrove to us, we found his lawyer's business card in his wallet. We called his lawyer the day after his operation, since we had no idea how to let anyone in his family know he was here. I guess the Police didn't bother to go through his stuff.

"No, they didn't," I say, sounding pissed off. "I had to call Lord knows how many Police stations and hospitals to find out where he was."

I walk around the room to Pops' bed and put my head on his chest and start sobbing like crazy.

"Baby, why did you have to come here? I told you not to go! Why did you leave me? I need you! We were supposed to get married in a few months, have our babies, and be together forever. This shit ain't fair!" I start screaming and fall to the floor.

Pops' Mom runs up to me, picks me up and hugs me. She tries to calm me down.

"Baby you can't change God's will, I miss him already. He's my son! I know it hurts, but we're going to get through this."

"What am I supposed to do, Doctor?" I look up at the doctor who's standing there looking at us like he wishes he could change things.

"I hate to do this right now, but I think you should get a hold of his lawyer, here is the card we found on him. You need to discuss the will. But as for right now, since we're here, I have to ask you, do you want to sign this form which gives us permission to pull the plug, since there is no chance of recovery for Mr Hardgrove. He will only suffer if you keep him alive and make your lives harder taking care of him and knowing he will never wake up. I'm sorry, if you need some time to think about it I understand. Here is my card; please let us know what you want to do."

"We will Doctor, thank you." I grab the card and put it in my purse.

"Mama, what do you want to do?" I look at her seriously.

She looks over at me, then at her son. She closes her eyes and says the words I have been waiting for.

"Landy, baby, go and get the doctor, I want to put my baby to rest in peace."

Mrs Hardgrove puts her arms around me and we cry until the Doctor and Landy come back.

"Doctor, we have decided to put my son to rest. I don't want him to suffer anymore."

"Alright, I need you to sign right here, Miss Crystal, then pull this plug." He points to the outlet.

Emilia Szleszynska

I sign the paper and stand next to the machine.

"Mama, you do it, I can't. I won't be able to live with myself." I walk away from the bed; Landy looks at me like I'm crazy. Like, 'what the hell are you waiting for'?

"I'm sorry, Miss, you have to be the one to pull the plug." The Doctor says, like I knew he would.

"Mama, can you at least do it with me, just put your hand on top of mine, please"

"If it's okay with the Doctor, baby." I look over at the doc.

"I guess that will be fine."

We both walk over to his bed. Mama leans over, kisses her son, and says her goodbyes. I do the same, and a part of me feels guilty that I'm happy to do this. But that guilt goes away pretty fast. We put our hands on the plug together, pull it, and watch the line go flat on the life support machine.

Finally my misery has ended. I start crying and run out of the room, Landy following behind me. I turn around in the hallway, hug her and say, smiling, "It's over, dog."

"Yes, it's over, and you didn't have anything to do with it."

"I had the pleasure of pulling the plug."

"That you did. Shh! Here comes Mama."

"Baby, it's going to be alright, he's in a better place. I'll make the funeral arrangements and get his body back to Detroit. You should call his lawyer and make an appointment about the will. My son must have really loved you to leave you everything."

"Everything? Like what?" I ask confused.

"Well, I'm sure you'll get both of the houses and the cars and, knowing Pops, he has stocks and bonds and cash, of course. He wasn't going to leave you broke, baby."

"Why wouldn't he leave it to you, Mama?"

"I'm set for the rest of my life, baby. My son made sure I would never need anything and now he's made sure you won't either." She says. "Let's go back to the room and get ready to leave. We've got a lot to do. I'll take care of everything far as the funeral goes, baby. You get a hold of the lawyer and the Police. See if they have any idea of who did this to my baby."

"Okay Mama, I love you. Let's leave this place. I've got to call my family too."

We get back in the car. Me and Landy go to my room, while Mom goes to hers.

"Let's pack up and bounce." I say as soon as we close the door.

"I've got to call this lawyer and see what he really left me."

"Shit, you didn't even have to get your hands dirty to get rid of his ass and you get paid for it!" Landy goes on about the jackpot I hit.

"God is good." I tell her, smiling, while I'm packing my shit.

"All the time," she says, smiling back and also packing.

"I've got to get Spin back, Landy, that's all I can think about. I'm ready to give all this shit up and let it go."

"Shit you might be able to with all the shit he's left you. With property value, you've got about a Mill Ticket! You ain't planning to keep both of those houses, are you?"

"Hell no, I ain't keeping nothing the bastard lived or drove in. All the shit is getting put up for sale tomorrow!" I sing the tomorrow part.

"Shit, you can lie back and chill and invest the shit in real estate or something."

"Trust me; I've got this, dog!" I smile and laugh at the same time. "I've got you too." I look over at my best friend and hug her, with tears in my eyes.

"You'd better, bitch" Landy says laughing.

"It's over. He is really gone." I close my suitcase and go towards the door and to the car.

"Let's stop by Mom's room and say bye. I've got to stick around for a minute at least until after the funeral and until I get his will signed over. Then I can work on getting my woman back."

"You think Spin is going to take your ass back?"

"Who wouldn't take me back?" I laugh while we're walking down the hallway to Mom's room.

"I wouldn't take your ass back if you played my ass like you did to her!"

"Bitch, please, yes you would! It's Spin we're talking about." I knock on the door while we both put on our sad faces.

"Hey baby, I'm ready to go too. I called the family. The body is being shipped today and I'll make all the arrangements once I get home." She closes the door.

Chapter 17:

Landy, Mrs Hardgrove, and me walk to our rental car and drive to the airport. A few hours later, back in the 'D', I pull off the freeway and hit Telegraph. I drop Pops' mom off, and then Landy and me are on our way to my mother's house. Home sweet home. We're going to spend the night there and meet with the lawyer tomorrow morning to go over the will. I finally pull up in the driveway. We get our bags and walk into the house. My whole damn family just happen to be home. I give them a quick version of what happened. They're all in shock, telling me how sorry they are and all the other shit I really don't care to hear, but I play along with it. They never really knew Pops, but they knew of him.

Finally, after dinner, I take Landy home and decide to call Spin. Some female answers the phone.

"May I speak to Spin please?"

"One second," she calls her name.

"Who's calling?" She asks.

"This is Vanilla." I say, aggravated.

Who is this chick? I think to myself.

"Hold on, Vanilla." She puts the phone down and ten seconds later Spin picks it up.

"Hello?!" She sounds annoyed.

"What's up, can I see you please? A lot of shit happened; I can't talk about it over the phone, if you don't mind can I come ov…."

"Stop, Crystal, I told you, there's nothing to talk about, it's over. Worry about your man, not me!"

"Pops is dead, Spin!"

"What? Damn, what did you do to the nigga?" She sounds shocked.

"What I did was pull the plug on his life support machine after he'd been shot six times in Chicago."

"I'm sorry, I guess." She says, sounding shocked.

"Girl, please, I'm gladder than anyone that he is gone and you should know that by now. I'm seeing his lawyer about the will tomorrow at 10:00am, he left everything to me."

"Damn somebody else did the dirty work and you got paid for it." She says, not sounding surprised.

"Yeah, that's what Landy said."

"Shit, she was right. How is she anyway?"

"She went to Chicago with me, I just dropped her off, and she's fine."

"Tell her I said, 'what's up'."

"I will. Please Spin, I need to see you baby! I'm begging. Come on, you know I don't beg!" I sound miserable.

"Please, Vanilla, you'd do anything to get what you want, no matter how dirty it is."

"Yeah, I would, especially when it comes to you." I say, smiling to myself. "I'll be there in about fifteen minutes."

"Alright."

"Hey Spin, who was that who answered the phone?"

"There you go already. It's my little cousin! Is that okay with you?"

"Yup. See you in a minute." I hang up, feeling relieved.

I know that as long as I see her, shit is going to be A1 from here. I pull up in front of her house, get out, walk up to the door, turn the door knob, and walk in. Spin is walking out of the kitchen with nothing but a bikini top on and little-ass shorts. She looks sexy as hell! My mind is imagining all the things I want to do to her.

"Are you just going to walk into my house like you live here?" She says, grabbing a shirt off the couch.

"I guess it's just a habit." I reply, not knowing what else to say.

"A habit you broke when you left, Vanilla."

"Please, Spin, let's not argue about this anymore."

"What? You expect me to act like this never happened?"

"No, but what is arguing going to do? He is dead, Spin! You don't understand how happy I am about that. He's dead and I've got everything he owns. It's like a dream come true, but I don't want any of it if I can't have you to share it with. I want to quit the business, and give this shit over to Sophia. I want to move out of Michigan with you and start over. We are set for life!"

"You think you can buy me, Crystal?"

"Shit, you act like I'm trying to buy you for a $100 or something! We've got over two million dollars worth of property, not to mention the money and bonds and stocks he's got in the bank! You can have all the shit Spin, but I don't want you to come back to me if you don't love me anymore. You do still love me, right?" I ask her, hoping she says what I want to hear so I didn't just make an ass out of myself.

Emilia Szleszynska

"Of course I love you. But you fucked me over so bad, and now your so-called man is dead, you expect me to just run back to you because he left you millions?"

"Yeah," I say, not knowing what else to say.

"Hell no, Crystal."

"Shit, if you ask me, you're stupid not to, Spin. You don't think you can forgive me?"

"Not this quick." She sits down and puts her head in her hands.

"Nobody said you've got to forgive me now, but let's try to work this out, please." I'm still begging. "Think about it, no more hoes, no more hustling, just you and me. We can go and finish school finally. We can do something legit with all this money. Just give it a chance, please."

"You're willing to quit the game for me?"

"Yes!" I scream and grab her hands in mine.

"No more hoes, just you and me?" She asks, smiling. "We can move to wherever I want to move?" She's really smiling now.

"As long as it's not too far from my family." I reply.

"Let's move to New York or something like that. I love you so much, Crystal, you know that, right?"

"Hell yeah! How can you not love this? I love you too, Mami. Always have, always will." I kiss her nose.

"I couldn't tell these last few months." She says, rolling her eyes.

"I know. I promise I will make it up to you." I start kissing her neck.

"Where's your little cousin?"

"She left before you got here."

"Good. I miss this pussy." I put my hands between her legs, under her shorts and like always she has nothing else on under there.

"Damn girl you're wet as hell."

"I'm horny as hell, that's why!" She giggles.

"Damn, I miss that!"

"You missed this, didn't you?" She asks me. I lie her on the couch, slowly take her shorts off, lift her sexy ass legs in the air and start licking her sweet ass pussy until she cums in my mouth.

"Damn, I miss this pussy; your shit is so hot and sweet. Who have you been fucking?"

"Shut up, Crystal. Who have *you* been fucking?"

"Shit, yours is the last pussy I tasted. The only pussy I want to taste!"

"What if we both want to fuck somebody?"

"That's on you, baby."

"I want to taste you too, Vanilla Ice Cream Cone!" I love when she calls me that!

"You will, we've got all night baby. I've got to go and see Pops' lawyer in the morning. The funeral is on Sunday. You know I've got to be there, right?"

"Yeah, I guess it won't look right if I go, huh?"

"No, not really; his family is going to be there and shit. I don't feel like explaining shit, it will only bring a lot of heat. I don't want to go, for real."

"I know you don't, baby."

"I want to go to your room now and make love to you, then hit the mall. What have you been doing for money?"

Emilia Szleszynska

"Living off my savings, and not buying Prada and Gucci; I've been looking for a good job."

"You can buy whatever you want now and you ain't going to get a damn job! You'll get to finish school and have your own law firm like you always wanted."

"What are you going to get?" She asks me.

"A little real estate, a car dealership, maybe a club," I laugh. "Anything we want baby. Right now, I want to hit that pussy."

"Come get it then." She looks at me seductively. She runs to the room, giggling, I'm about to beat it up with a strap on then let her do me. I miss her eating this pussy. I've finally got my baby back.

After a few hours of love making we hit the mall. I hook my baby up with 7 G's worth of clothes and everything else she needs. Then we hit the movies and I take her out to dinner. We talk about everything that's been going on in her life and about our future, trying to leave the past behind. We make it an early night, no clubbing. I've got too much business to take care of in the morning. We get back to the crib and make love all damn night.

Chapter 18:

The alarm clock wakes me up at 8:15am. I jump up, take a shower, and put on the new suit I bought yesterday at the mall. I also bought myself a new black Chanel suit for the funeral. Something special for one of the best days of my life!

I wake Spin up at 9:00am; I'm ready to leave out. I've got to meet the lawyer at 10:00am.

"Baby, I'll be back in a few hours, okay? I've got to go and see this lawyer. I love you." I lean over and kiss her on the cheek.

"Okay, love you too." She rolls over and covers her face with the silk Gucci sheets. I just laugh and walk out the door.

On my drive to the lawyer's office, I call Sophia and tell her I've got a present for her and I want her to meet me at Spin's house at about 2:00pm. She sounds surprised and confused. I tell her it's a good surprise and not to worry about it.

I pull up in front of the lawyer's office; it's a nice, private practice. I see Pops' Mom's car parked next to a Land Rover. She got here early. I walk in. She's talking to the secretary. I walk up to her and touch her shoulder to let her know I'm there. She looks terrible. I feel sorry for her for a minute; that was her baby.

"Hey Mama," I kiss her on the cheek.

"Hey baby. Good, you're here, let's get this over with so I can bury my son in peace."

"We don't have to rush things, Mama. I want to make sure you are comfortable with everything, I know this is hard on you, trust me, it's hard on me too."

"I would give it all up just to have him back." I look at her with tears in my eyes and, when I try to hug her, my head spins and I seen lights and everything turns black. I grab her shoulder for support and finally, after what seems like forever, my head stops spinning. I am able to see and hear the fuss Mom was making over me.

"Somebody get me some water!" She screams at the secretary.

"Baby, sit down, what's wrong? You need to go to the doctors!"

"No, I'm fine, just tired. I haven't had much sleep, that's all; it was just a dizzy spell."

"If you want we can reschedule this, Miss. You should get some rest." This comes from a man standing behind me. I look up and see the face of an older black man in his sixties. He's very handsome. Damn, what am I doing checking this dude out? This must be the lawyer.

"No need. We need to get this over with so everybody can put this behind them. I'm fine. I'll go home and get some sleep right after this, Mama, I promise."

"Okay baby, but you'd better go to the doctors just to make sure you're alright."

"I'll make an appointment, I promise. I'm sorry, you must be the lawyer, I'm Crystal, Pops' wife, and you are?"

"Just call me Jerome. This way please, Mrs Hardgrove. This shouldn't take long since I've had a few days to go over the paper work. You are going to be one rich young woman, Miss Crystal."

"Not without Pops." I say really low and grab Mrs Hardgrove's hand. "Please don't let me hold you up; I'm sure you have other things to do." I tell the lawyer, trying to get out of here A.S.A.P.

I know, I've got other things to do, I think to myself.

"Oh no, this is my job, Pops paid me well to take care of his business. Please sit down." He points to two chairs across from his desk. Jerome finally sits down behind the desk and goes through a folder which I suppose is Pops' will.

"Okay, let's start this with Mrs Hardgrove. To you, Pops left all of his real estate properties, and I guess you already have the money transferred to your account from the way this looks?"

"Yes, me and Pops took care of this a few months back." She says looking at the lawyer and then me.

"Since we're here, I would like to sign the real estate properties over to Crystal. I'm too old to take care of that, plus I don't know anybody who has better business sense than her."

"Mrs Hardgrove?" I say, sounding shocked. "Are you serious?"

"He would want you to have it before anybody else, baby."

"Thank you. I promise to do the right thing with it. How much are they worth? The properties, I mean." I ask the lawyer.

"An estimated 2.7 million," he smiles.

"What?" I sound shocked.

"He has a lot of properties. I'll give you the deeds to all the properties by next week. I need you to sign these over in her name, Mrs Hardgrove."

"Where do I sign?" She picks up the pen.

"Right here," he points to a line, she signs, and then Jerome gives me the paper and asks me to sign below it.

I do it fast as hell, before she changes her mind. I can't believe she just signed over 2.7 million worth of property to me!

"Is this property in usc right now?"

"Yes it is, Miss. You have a few apartment buildings, a few offices, a couple of houses and a club, which Pops was going to open November 5th this year. It's called *Vanilla's Ladies.*"

"That's my birthday and that's my nickname, he named the club after me?"

"It was supposed to be your birthday present." His Mom tells me, smiling.

"Oh my god," I put my hand over my mouth, shocked.

"I know I did the right thing signing this over to you. What would I do with a club?" Mom's trying to laugh a little.

"If you stop by my office some time by the end of this week we can go over all the paper work and properties and what Pops had in mind with the club. Just call me and we'll make an appointment."

"That sounds good, thank you, Jerome. By the way, if it's okay with you, I would like to hire you as my lawyer, since you already know all the ropes and know exactly what Pops wanted to do with everything."

"I was hoping you would keep me around. It will be my pleasure to guide you in your investments. Thank you, Miss." We shake hands.

"You're welcome." I smile and get up. "Now, when it comes to the rest of the will, everything else belongs to you, which is the three homes Mr Hardgrove had in Michigan. I'm sure you're familiar with the locations?"

"Yes, I am."

"There is also a beach house in Jamaica, a 210 foot yacht worth 1.2 million, 1.9 million in cash and over $700,000 in jewellery."

"Oh my god!" I say sounding more shocked than ever before.

"I'll do all the transfers this week. Everything will be ready by the end of the week when we meet to deal with the properties. Any other questions?" He looks at both of us. I'm still shocked about how much money he left me. I guess it was worth the ass whoopings I got. "Here's my card, please feel free to call me if you need anything Mrs Hardgrove, you too Miss Crystal."

"Thank you, I will" I say, shaking his hand again and getting ready to bounce.

"Thank you again, Jerome." Mom hugs him and we walk out of the office.

I kiss Mom and promise to keep in touch, and go to the doctor. I get in the car and call Spin before I pull off.

"We're so rich, bitch!!! I mean stupid-ass rich! Millions of dollars rich! Yacht and private condo in Jamaica rich! Real estate worth millions rich!"

"Oh my god!" Is all she can say, then she starts screaming.

"Call Sophia for me and tell her she can have the damn business and every hoe that comes with it, except you."

"I'm a hoe now?" She says, trying to sound mad and doing a very bad job of it.

"Not anymore!" I laugh and hang up.

"Life is a bitch, and then you get rich!" I say to myself and put in some 2-Pac.

I cruise all the way to Spin's house. We are celebrating tonight. I'm a fucking millionaire at 19! Maybe now I can be an actress, or have my own T.V. show. I'll be the next Oprah. No, I ain't *that* rich.

I pull up in front of Spin's crib, jump out and run to the door. She opens it before I get a chance to and before I know it, I fall straight on Spin.

"Vanilla, what's wrong with you? Are you alright?" I hear Spin yelling, but I can't answer.

Finally she walks me to the couch, my head stops spinning and I'm able to see.

"Damn, that is the second time this shit has happened today, I've got to go and see a doctor!" I say looking at Spin.

"Yes, you do, we're going right now."

"Wait a minute, I've got to call my family first and let them know about the will. Call my doctor and see if she can fit me in today. Did you call Sophia?"

"Yes, she's on her way over here. I didn't tell her everything. I just told her you've got some good news for her."

"Good, I want to tell her myself, just to see the look on her face."

"She's going to flip out!" Spin tells me, then walks up to me and kisses me.

"Give me your doctor's number."

"Hold on, let me get the business card out my purse." I dig in my purse, pull the card out and hand it to her.

"Tell her this has happened twice today, it's just a dizzy spell, I see lights and blackness for a few seconds and get really weak."

"Alright, let me get you some water first."

"Thank you, baby, I love you!" I yell behind her.

"Yeah, I know, I love you to, Ma!" Someone knocks on the door.

I walk to the door, look through the peep hole, and open the door to let Sophia in.

"What's up, V? This better be good. You've got me all anxious and shit!"

"Just shut up and sit down!" I tell her, laughing. She sits down.

Spin brings me my water, hugs Sophia and I give her what she has been trying to get from me since day one.

"Since Pops left me enough money and property to be tight for the rest of my life, I've decided that I'm ready to let you run the service from now on."

"What do you mean? I'm running it for you now?" She says sounding confused.

"I mean you can have the service, and everything that comes with it. I'm going to sign my business license over to you. All the girls can stay and work if they want. I don't want shit else to do with it."

"I ... I ... I can't believe you are giving it to me and not Spin!" Sophia says sounding shocked.

"Spin is with me. She's not going to need shit. Just so she knows, I will never play her like I did before. I'm opening bank account for her as soon as the money gets transferred to my account in a few days. I've got to make an appointment with my lawyer sometime this week to sign all these damn papers. His Mom even signed over the real estate properties he left her. He was opening a club on my birthday called *Vanilla's Ladies*. I'll get all the details later, but I've got to go and see my doctor now. What time does she want me to be there, Spin?"

"She said just to come in before 4:00pm."

"Alright, I'm about to stop by the crib and then I'll go to see the Doc."

"Why are you going to see a Doctor? Are you alright?" Sophia asks, looking worried.

"I keep on getting dizzy and seeing lights and having hot flashes and passing out. It's probably stress and I'm tired as hell."

"I'll call you as soon as I see her, I love you baby." I kiss Spin and hug Sophia. I go to the car and head to my Mom's crib to tell her she never has to work another day in her life, unless she wants to and, knowing her, she will. I have never been so glad to leave my mother's house! They just went crazy! Spending the money before I even get my hands on it!

Pops must be turning over in his grave right now, wishing he had changed his will. Too late! In a funny way, I do miss him, but I'm so glad he's gone! Never again will I let anything come between me and Spin.

Epilogue:

I pull up in front of Doctor Ozog's office, park and go in. I sign in, and let the receptionist know I'm there. I tell her that I don't have an appointment as it's an emergency and I'm paying cash. That was the magic word.

"She will see you in a few minutes, Miss."

"Okay, thank you." I sit down and grab a magazine.

Before I know it she calls my name.

"Crystal? The doctor will see you now." I jump up and walk in.

"So, tell me what's wrong with you, Crystal?"

"Hell, I thought that was *your* job?" I say playfully and laugh.

"That was a good one." She smiles and checks my pulse, temperature and all the other shit.

"I want a urine sample. Your vitals are fine. Is there a chance you may be pregnant?"

"I'm gay, doc."

"Well, have you had sex with a man in the last few weeks?"

"Well, yes, but I'm on the damn pill. I mess up taking it once in a while, but I make up for it the next day. Plus, he just got murdered; I can't be pregnant right now. I never even thought about that being the reason I'm feeling sick! Let me see the cup, I know it's got to be something else."

I go to the bathroom and come out with a sample. I give it to her and wait, nervous as hell, while she dips the stick in it. Those were the longest three minutes of my life.

"Well Crystal, you're definitely pregnant."

"You've got to be kidding?" I jump out my seat and start pacing the room. "I can't be! I don't want to be!" I start panicking and sit back down, get back up, sit back down, then get up again.

I grab my purse and storm out of the office. I get in the car in the biggest daze I have ever been in in my life on my way back to Spin's house.

I pull up, jump out the car, and run into the house. Spin is looking at me like I'm crazy, which I feel right now.

"What's wrong? What the hell did the doctor say? Are you okay? Damn it, Vanilla, talk to me!" She yells at me now.

I snap back to myself.

"I'm pregnant, Spin! I'm fucking pregnant with that bastard's child!" I go to the kitchen, grab some water and down half the bottle.

"Calm down, Crystal, calm down. Think about it, it might not be such a bad thing. We can have this baby, you and me. We can raise this baby, this can be *our* baby. The only good thing that nigga could give us, other than the money."

"What's wrong with you, Spin?"

"You're in shock right now; calm down, think about it, V. Don't you want a baby?"

"Yeah, but not with him!"

"He's dead for Christ sake, Vanilla! This baby is a blessing, damn it! You're lucky you can have fucking kids!" I'm shocked she's so emotional about this. I just look at her in a daze.

"Not everyone can! *I* can't have kids, Crystal, that was the main reason I started fucking with women, because I always felt no man would want to marry me. Who would want me to be their wife when I can't even give them children? Plus, the fact that I already liked women made it easier. So you should feel blessed! Have this baby for us, for me." She grabs my hand, puts in on my stomach and we both start crying.

"Baby, I'm sorry, I didn't know; why didn't you ever tell me you couldn't have kids?"

"It's not something I like to talk about, okay?"

"We're going to have this baby, okay? This is going to be our baby, not Pops', okay Mama?"

"I love you Crystal." I look at her pretty face and tell her how I feel.

"I love you too, Mami. Look, the funeral is tomorrow." I say. "Should I tell his Mom I'm pregnant?"

"That's up to you," Spin looks at me, smiling. "She does have the right to know. It would be good to have extra grandparents, plus it will make her happy knowing her only son left her a grandchild. She lost a son, but at the same time, got a piece of him back on the day she buried him!" Spin says to me smiling.

"You're right. Just wait until I tell my parents, they're going to freak out. Call the lawyer and tell him I want to meet him tomorrow afternoon, here's the card." I hand her his business card.

"I'm about to go and see Mom, I'll be back here tonight. I love you baby."

"I love you too, Vanilla."

I get to my parents house and tell them what happened. They take the news as a surprise, but are very pleased about it since they think I'm happy to have a part of Pops left. In a way I am, maybe more for Spin than myself. And his family are even happier.

This is going to be weird, but I'm not going to say I ever regretted meeting him or going through what I went through. Once the funeral is over with, me and Spin get to move away somewhere far from here for a minute, or at least until the baby is born. I need some peace. I'll quit, start my life over, put my sister in charge of the new club, finish school, and live the good life thanks to the man who tried to ruin my life. Life's a bitch, then you get rich! (Well, some of us do. Some of us die. R.I.P. Pops)